Strange Sisters

The Art of Lesbian Pulp Fiction
1949-1969

With a foreword by Ann Bannon

JAYE ZIMET

VIKING STUDIO

VIKING STUDIO
Published by the Penguin Group
Penguin Putnam Inc., 375 Hudson
Street, New York, New York 10014,
U.S.A.; Penguin Books Ltd, 27 Wrights
Lane, London W8 5TZ, England; Penguin
Books Australia Ltd, Ringwood, Victo-
ria, Australia; Penguin Books Canada
Ltd, 10 Alcorn Avenue, Toronto, Ontario,
Canada M4V 3B2; Penguin Books (N.Z.)
Ltd, 182-190 Wairau Road, Auckland
10, New Zealand

Penguin Books Ltd, Registered Offices:
Harmondsworth, Middlesex, England

First published in 1999 by Viking Studio, a member of Penguin Putnam Inc.

1   3   5   7   9   10   8   6   4   2

Cover art for *Libido Beach* by Alain
Abby, *Reformatory Girls* by Ray Morri-
son, *Voyage from Lesbos* by Richard
Robertiello, *House of Fury* by Felice
Swados, and *The Scorpion* by A. E.
Weirach reproduced by permission of
Avon Books, Inc. Cover art for *American
Sexual Behavior* by Morris Ernst and
David Roth, *The Mesh* by Lucie Marchal,
and *The Price of Salt* by Claire Morgan
reproduced by permission of Bantam
Books, a division of Random House,
Inc. Cover art for *Women* edited by A.
M. Krich reproduced by permission of
Dell Publishing, a division of Random
House, Inc. Definition of "strange" from
*Merriam-Webster's Collegiate® Dictio-
nary,* 10th edition. © 1999 by Merriam-
Webster, Incorporated. Used by
Permission.

CIP   data   available

ISBN: 0-14-028402-8

PRINTED ON ACID-FREE PAPER
∞

PRINTED   IN   U.   S.   A.

SET   IN   FUTURA   BOLD
DESIGNED BY JAYE ZIMET

AUTHOR'S NOTE
Artist credits where known are provided in the captions. The absence of a cover credit or signature
makes positive identification difficult, though I have attempted to identify the cover artist from other
sources. Where I could not verify the artist through any source, no artist credit is given. All books il-
lustrated are from my own collection.

for Stephanie

Contents

Foreword | 9

Introduction | 17

Women Alone | 27

Positive Portraits | 45

Dangerous Desires | 91

Longing Looks | 103

Bi, Bi, Love | 119

Strange Sisters | 61

Cliterature | 71

Psycho-Babble | 83

Cleavage | 127

Sleaze | 139

Bibliography | 151

Resources | 153

Index | 155

Acknowledgments | 159

Foreword

Who are these "girls"? Gazing at the pulp-art covers of the lesbian fiction published half a century ago is like reconnecting with old acquaintances; I hesitate to call them friends, since I never really recognized them as such. In fact, over the years as my own books were published, I looked in astonishment at the choices the editors and art directors had made. The books arrived in plain brown packets, for the very good reason that they were deliberately evocative of shady sex. With only small adjustments, and sometimes none at all, the young women I was looking at could easily have walked off those pulp covers and onto the pages of *Harper's Bazaar* to sell the "New Look." Many could have graced the ladies' undies section of the Sears, Roebuck catalog just as they were. In their various transformations, they bore scant resemblance to the girls I had written about—and we *did* call them "girls" in those ingenuous days.

Still, they had a kind of appeal. Without intending to, the artists and photographers could sometimes imbue them with a sort of wistfulness, as if they were wondering "What am I doing on this cover? Is this any place for a nice girl?" In the case of a cover photograph, I often felt rather sorry for the young woman looking up at the reader. She was clearly intended to appeal to the large male readership, and not to the lesbian constituency that we women writers, at least, thought we were reaching out to. What in the world did the photographers say to the women who were expected to project this ambiguous charm? I have a theory that perhaps they made the assumption so often made in respect to children's textbooks: *if we can make this interesting for the boys, we don't need to worry about the girls. The boys will accept them, and the girls won't have any choice. The girls always go along anyway.*

To be fair, and as we recognized even then, there are some lesbians who really do look glamorous, and like it that way. Remember the "femmes" of seductive memory? And think of today's analogous charmers: "lipstick lesbians." It was the absence of those wonderful dykes with the broad shoulders that we missed. Whatever the strategy, and despite the almost comical disconnect between the covers and the contents, the books found both their intended audiences.

Authors were the last people consulted by the editors about pulp fiction covers, and probably for good reason. We knew what our characters looked like and wanted to see them materialize on our book covers. We cared intensely about the effect the cover designs would have on the readership. The editors, however, knew something more practical: how to move their inventory. If it took a cutie in Frederick's of Hollywood scanties, that's what we got. If it took two pretty girls naughtily smoking, drinking, and glaring—at each other or some sorry male—we got that. If it took one pretty young woman looking straight as a pine tree, gingerly patting the hair of another, equally squirmy and misplaced young heterosexual female, never mind. At least it sold the books.

In my own case, after a string of five covers that ranged from peculiar to surreal, from 1930s-style magazine illustration to 1960s-type art photography, you can imagine the state of mind in which I waited to see the cover of my last Gold Medal book: *Beebo Brinker.* Half in dread, half in hope I wondered: what had the artist and the editor perpetrated? What gulf would exist between my Beebo and theirs? *My* Beebo was tall, strong, handsome—and blue-jeaned. Theirs ... well, those of you who can recall that original cover must have wondered if the editors had read the book—as indeed, the cover artists seldom did. *Beebo Brinker* did at last arrive. I tore open the brown paper packet, hoping mainly for some intelligent compromise: she would be tall and handsome, but perhaps, as a newcomer to the big city, wearing her traveling clothes of skirt and blazer. But there would be something sturdy and defiant and captivating about her, something boyishly rugged and profoundly female. You would know at once that, young and naïve she might be, but a joyful, witty, sexy woman in the making, nonetheless. I studied the cover. It was really the only time I found myself in *The Twilight Zone* over one of my own books. There gazing back at me was a skinny, scared, adolescent girl with a page boy bob, wearing brown broughams and white bobby socks—a fusty fashion disaster, even by the teenage standards of that time. The figure stood under a street light in what passed for Greenwich Village, adopting the famous—even then—"debutante slouch," and looking for all the world like a kid who had come to make it as a fashion model, but who needed an industrial-strength makeover. As covers went, it was a megabomb. Interestingly, however, it was the only one of my books, and one of the few from this whole interesting category, whose cover had not been crafted to appeal to that most durable of male fantasies: female-on-female sex.

And speaking of clothes, where did all those pink tap pants come from? Those fluffy negligees? Those peach silk slips? In those days, real girls wore 100 percent cotton "lollipop" briefs, plain white. They provided coverage even our grandmothers could approve, from above the navel to below the buns. No need to wax the bikini line. None of those lacy pushup things, either. Bras were of sturdy cotton, circle-stitched so as to give our breasts no-nonsense conical points. Indeed, they appeared to be aimed fatally at anyone who got closer than three feet. As for outerwear, many of the covers exhibit young women in torn blouses, unbuttoned blouses, sheer blouses, and the occasional peignoir—standard issue, of course, for all self-respecting lesbians of the 1950s and 1960s.

What was the goal? Again, it was the calculated and clever representation of female gender displayed as an incentive to the boys to buy the book.

It is true that many books were written and sold as "lesbian fiction" during the heyday of the pulps, that were, in fact, written by men using female pseudonyms. And male readers had no difficulty finding them. But by far the largest number was written by and for women. Given the off-putting covers, so clearly meant to serve as come-ons to a male readership, how did women identify these books? What was it like to walk into a drugstore, a train station, a newsstand and see a lavishly endowed young sexpot primping on the cover of something called *Women's Passions* while she was ogled by another babe in a state of undress? In a word: awkward. Even scary.

Because, despite all the care devoted to developing cover art that would activate male gonads, women learned to recognize what was a nascent literature of their own by reading the covers iconically. If there was a solitary woman on the cover, provocatively dressed, and the title conveyed her rejection by society or her self-loathing, it was a lesbian book. If there were two women on the cover, and they were touching each other (we're not talking mother and daughter here, of course), it was a lesbian book. Even if they were just looking at each other; even if they were simply in proximity to one another; even if they were merely on the same cover together, it was reason to hope you had found a lesbian book. And if a lone male, whether looking embarrassed, hostile, or sexually deprived, appeared with two women, you had probably struck gold. Perhaps even more than the cover illustrations, the titles were classic giveaways, my own included. *Women in the Shad-*

ows, Odd Girl Out, and even worse, *I Am a Woman in Love with a Woman: Must Society Re-ject Me?* (We weren't allowed to choose our titles, either.) But bad as they were, the titles did signal the content. I would regret their awkwardness and utter lack of subtlety, but some of them had a peculiar poetry of their own. By and large, they served their purpose—the promise of a lesbian love story between the covers. But buying them? The difficult part was to screw up one's courage to carry a pile of these spicy titles and unmistakable illustrations to a drugstore counter, covers gleaming with neon prurience, and survive the smirk as the cashier rang them up. One had to hope that no acquaintance lurked nearby to carry tales to re-spectable friends and relations. It was essential to plan in advance where to hide one's liter-ary stash, away from the risk of familial judgment: under the mattress? In the socks drawer? Behind the fridge? Wherever, it had to fool snooping eyes.

Despite all their editorially imposed quirks, the covers provided links among members of a wide-flung and incohesive community; a community that did not even think of itself as one and that, therefore, valued all the more any connection with others whose experience paral-leled their own.

It is notable that there was little analogous "gay pulp fiction" in the era of the fifties and sixties. There were a few books of "serious" fiction, which dealt with men's homosexuality, most of them published in France by Olympia Press and other, similar operations. Unless they were medical texts, they were often contraband in the United States. Male homosexuality had a potentially large read- 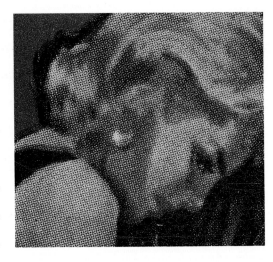 ership among the extensive gay community, but no cultural consensus that it, too, was beautiful and a worthy subject for fiction. Nor was there an obvious and eager audience of women aroused by male-on-male lovemaking. It was not that they didn't exist but that such a phenomenon, in parallel to that of men reading lesbian fiction, was unimaginable in that era. No editor would have credited the notion or willingly committed professional suicide to launch a movement of gay pulp fiction. Still, it is intriguing to imagine what *those* covers might have been like: two men in a military barracks, half dressed, one gazing somnolently at the other. A boy in a torn T-shirt, revealing manly décolletage, looking provocatively at the reader as he lounges, smoking, on a bed. A guy in jeans, bare-chested, bending away from the viewer, crack in full view, while a male bystander in a shadowed doorway checks him out appreciatively. It might have been tasteless, but it would have been fun.

If I were young today, I would be tempted to pass judgment a bit unkindly on the covers of pulp fiction novels from the 1950s and 1960s. What were they thinking, those editors, artists, and authors, of that faraway era? This is false and misleading advertising. Were times really so bad that they couldn't strive for some semblance of honesty?

But in fact we were trying to be honest *between* the covers. In large numbers, we were speaking to an audience of women who were starved for connections with others, who thought they were uniquely alone with emotions they couldn't explain and couldn't find mirrored in their own worlds. In our way, we held up that mirror—not always a perfect reflection, alas, but often a comforting one. We were in the vanguard of what later became a proud and brave social movement, and an honest one, too.

There have been many wonderful lesbian novels in the years since the pulps went out of publication, and they have been afforded covers that match their contents in appropriate ways. Even my own books, in a Naiad Press reissue, took on a far more seemly look. But surely I am not the only one who remembers with a twinge of nostalgia and affection the flowering of the lesbian pulps with those improbable but titillating women on the covers. We knew how to find them and how to read them. They reassured us of the potential in an apparently hostile world for affirming friendships, courage, and support. Jaye Zimet has made us all a gift of memory, both for those who lived through the era and for those who will preserve it in the history books.

—Ann Bannon

Introduction

It has been said that one cannot judge a book by its cover; however, that is precisely the intent of this book. Paperback book covers are an often disregarded slice of pop culture and a window into the interests, tastes and social attitudes of the time in which they were published. They provide a voyeuristic peek into exciting, sleazy, and often illicit worlds. Adjectives abound when describing pulp fiction covers—lurid, lewd, salacious, sensational, risqué. This is especially true of books featuring sexual encounters between two women. In this subgenre of lesbian pulp fiction, women were portrayed as sexually heightened creatures—some shameful or reluctant, some coy and alluring, some predatory, voracious and powerful—but all were presented for the vicarious pleasure of the viewer.

The mass-market paperback book originated in 1939 with the Pocket Book edition of Pearl S. Buck's *The Good Earth,* but the paperback explosion really started after World War II. During the war, GIs had access to government-issued paperback books, Armed Forces Editions, designed to fit into uniform pockets, that offered a broad range of literature, including a variety of popular fiction. In the decade following the war, publishers took advantage of this taste for novels written with a gritty realism: adventure stories, detective fiction, mysteries, and westerns.

Another factor feeding the paperback boom in postwar America was the newfound freedom that many women enjoyed. The war effort was powered by thousands of formerly dependent housewives looking to do their part. They worked alongside secretaries, sales clerks, and waitresses in industrial jobs once reserved for men. Rosie the Riveter was the predominant female icon at the time—patriotic, strong and independent. The cities were crowded with working women, and huge numbers stayed there after the war, continuing to live and work on their own. In the books they read, they sought a more realistic and diverse portrayal of women that reflected their own changing lives. The paperback boom in the 1950s was inevitable, given the changing tastes in fiction and the expansion of the suburbs with their plethora of labor-saving devices that suddenly created leisure time to fill with books, magazines, movies and television.

America's exposure to a more diverse range of sexuality also occurred during the war, with GIs loose overseas and women left unchaperoned in the big cities. A wide variety of sexuality has always been a part of the human experience, but was usually left unacknowledged publicly. That changed in 1948 when Dr. Alfred Kinsey published *Sexual Behavior of the Human Male*, followed by *Sexual Behavior of the Human Female* in 1951. Collectively known as the Kinsey Report, these studies openly confronted middle America with scientific evidence of the existence of a large spectrum of sexuality, including what was considered a high instance of homosexuality.

This is the paradox of the Eisenhower/McCarthy era: straitlaced suburban sensibility at one extreme and postwar freedom, excitement and sexual exploration at the other. Young people born in the 1930s started an explosion of teenage counterculture after the war that included the birth of rock 'n' roll and the emergence of the Beat generation. The media began to reflect and exploit their revolutionary behavior. Naturally, the publishing industry joined in and this blossomed into a whole genre of juvenile delinquency books. They in turn fed a broader range of fiction exploiting deviant behavior of all sorts; books sensationalizing sex, drugs and illegal or salacious activity of every kind found their way onto the paperback racks, their titles and cover art fighting each other for attention. The titles were direct and startling: *12 Chinks and a Woman; Marihuana; Junkie; I Killed Stalin; Jailbait; Hitch-Hike Hussy; I Am a Lesbian.*

With the increasing output of exploitational literature, the paperback industry saw attempts at censorship. In 1952, the U.S. House of Representatives appointed the Select Committee on Current Pornographic Materials. One of the exhibits selected was Tereska Torres's *Women's Barracks,* published by Fawcett under the Gold Medal imprint, which coincidentally became a bestseller. This was the first of a long stream of Gold Medal books having lesbian characters and situations. While their distribution company, Signet, limited the amount of reprints from hardcovers it could produce, Fawcett began to publish original material. In fact, its biggest contribution to the publishing industry was the paperback original, or PBO. This opened the door for a wide variety of material. Fawcett offered advances of two or three thousand dollars and manuscripts came pouring in, most from first-time authors. One of those authors was a Fawcett secretary, Marijane Meaker. Looking to take advantage of the success of *Women's Barracks,* Fawcett editor Dick Carroll asked Meaker if there was any homosexuality at her boarding school, to which she replied, "Sure, and a lot more of it at my sorority in college." He proposed that she write about that for the new paperback original line, with the only restriction being that it couldn't have a happy ending. Meaker's *Spring Fire* was published in 1952 under the pseudonym of Vin Packer. The book instantly became a multimillion-copy bestseller, reportedly outselling *God's Little Acre,* also published that year.

Women's Barracks made an impact, but *Spring Fire* started the trend. While it offered a relatively sincere and realistic account of a lesbian relationship, in the end, one woman goes off with her former beau and the other is committed to a mental hospital, establishing an important convention of the genre. According to Meaker, it was Dick Carroll who suggested that the lesbian go crazy in the end—"otherwise the post office might seize the books as obscene." Another author of original lesbian fiction for Gold Medal was Ann Bannon. After reading *Spring Fire, she* wrote to Meaker, who encouraged her to send in her own manuscript, which she eventually did and that was published in

1957 as *Odd Girl Out.* She, too, noted in an interview for the 1992 documentary film *Forbidden Love* that there must be an unhappy ending. "There was some kind of retribution that

was essential at the end so that you could let them have a little fun in the meantime and entertain the reader." Paula Christian, another Gold Medal author, had similar thoughts: "... It should be understood that a publisher cannot allow this theme to be promoted as something to be admired or desired."

The most remarkable thing was that almost all of the Gold Medal books with lesbian themes were written by women, most of whom were lesbians themselves. Other publishers soon followed with lesbian-themed books, but most were written by men under feminine or nongender-specific pen names.

The success of the lesbian pulp was in part due to the fact that they were targeted to the "prurient interests of men." But Marijane Meaker received hundreds of letters attesting to the strong readership of women. Because this was often the only literature with lesbian content available to gay women at the time, they had to read between the lines and ignore the homophobic and moralistic story lines. But they were rewarded to find some sensitive portraits of lesbian characters and nuggets of gay life in the 1950s. According to Ann Bannon, "There was a Golden Age of lesbian writing and publication that came to pass in the fifties and sixties, and I think that we suddenly reached out and connected with women who were very isolated and sequestered, almost, in little towns across the country. I think maybe that's one reason the paperback originals that did deal with the lesbian theme became so valuable to so many women. They were widely distributed and they said this is how it is, this is who some of your sisters are." Many of those books are still readable today, although one has to make allowances for the 1950s sensibility and censorship issues. As Ann Bannon points out about her work, "The books as they stand have fifties' flaws. They are, in effect, the offspring of their special era, with its biases. But they speak truly of that time and place as I knew it."

In the 1960s, while the sexual revolution was in full progress, the publishing industry produced quite a bit of "sleaze," including much lesbiana. Sleaze, essentially soft-core pornography, was often poorly written and was highly exploitational in its portrayal of women. These books were issued by adult-oriented publishing houses with very limited distribution, and they focused almost exclusively on sexual themes, although they usually avoided explicit depictions of sex to avoid obscenity charges. In contrast, the more mainstream publishing houses generally upheld a certain level of quality in writing and production.

Mainstream or sleaze, the cover drew attention to a book. The style of painting was drawn from the dimestore pulp digest magazines that the paperback was fast replacing. In fact, many of the paperback illustrators got their start doing work for the pulp mags. They were done in a hyperrealistic style and featured curvaceous women, scantily clad, whose overt sexuality dripped off the cover. The coy looks and titillating poses teased the male libido. Books with lesbian content were often, but not always, conspicuous. Sometimes the title or tag line was enough, but often one just had to look for two women on the cover, with at least one of them looking dreamily at the other. Lesbians picked up on the sometimes subtle clues from the cover art. One woman interviewed for *Forbidden Love* stated it this way: "The books were displayed with the other books, with mysteries and westerns and everything, and you had to dig to find them. The only way you could identify them was by the pictures on the covers. As soon as I'd see a picture of two women, I said, 'Oh, yes, that had to be one!' Grab! Grab!"

Cover artists often exaggerated misconceptions and stereotypes in their paintings, and with lesbians, that came down to the butch/femme dynamic. The butch is depicted with short hair, almost always brown or black, occasionally red. She can be portrayed as pretty, as on Robert Maguire's covers, but is often not. She wears pants when she can, but a plain skirt and blouse or basic underwear is also allowed. She always strikes a dominant position; i.e., standing over or above the other woman. One of my favorite butches is depicted on the cover of *Queer Beach*, page 148. The femme is usually blond, with long or shoulder-length hair, attractive and fully made up. She wears a low-cut dress, halfway unbuttoned blouse or lingerie, with as much cleavage showing as possible. She is the sex object who is displayed sitting or reclining, looking up into her lover's eyes. The more suggestive the scene, the better. Sometimes, one woman looks out seductively at the viewer, just asking to be picked up and handled. She may be called a *lesbian* but she probably is just waiting for the right man to come along to set her straight.

Often the women on the covers were nothing like what the author had written them to be. As Ann Bannon explains in her foreword, the cover of *Beebo Brinker* was a great disappoint-

ment. Bannon writes her as a strict butch, direct and no nonsense. "... she was proud of her size, proud of her strength, even proud of her oddly boyish face." The girl on the cover is looking slightly vulnerable, "just off the bus," so to speak, and wears a skirt suit and has a feminine hairdo—certainly not the stereotypical image of a butch in the 1950s. Pants and short hair were *de rigueur*.

While some publishers tried to tone down the cover art because of possible government censorship, overall the art grew more provocative in the early 1960s, and the sleaze covers became even more outrageous. However, the more lewd and lascivious the cover painting, the more likely the content was to disappoint the reader expecting a certain thrill. Women were often painted in the worst light. Clichés were rife, as lesbians were linked with all sorts of perverse or illegal activity. Often portrayed as sexual predators, no form of depravity was too low to be linked with lesbianism—satanism, sadism and masochism, bondage and disci-

pline, orgies, voyeurism, witchcraft. Two of the frequently exploited clichés were that when women were without men, they were bound to be turned into lesbians or that one dyke alone could corrupt any number of innocent young girls. Publishers and cover artists delighted in the depictions of lesbians in prison, in sororities, in dormitories and in reform schools, all waiting to seduce the newest addition.

This book presents 200 lesbian paperback book covers from the 1950s and 1960s. From realistic and emotionally resonant portrayals to laughably outrageous caricatures—at once naïve and nostalgic, seductive and sensational. Today, these covers are a source of campy amusement, a quaintly erotic journey into a world where women's sexuality is on display and available for anyone's enjoyment.

Strange Sisters

Women Alone

Judging from the visual clues on these covers, when women are segregated from men, lesbianism is the result. Some are born that way, some are coerced, but always with equally unhappy results. In prison, predatory females roam the halls in the form of inmates and wardens, as "bad girls" get what they deserve. In college dorms, there is always some dyke waiting to corrupt a pretty young co-ed. In the army, at school, at parties and at summer camp, these books often told of the horrors awaiting the naïve and unsuspecting. In the end, the lesbian gets her due . . . marriage, insanity or . . . suicide.

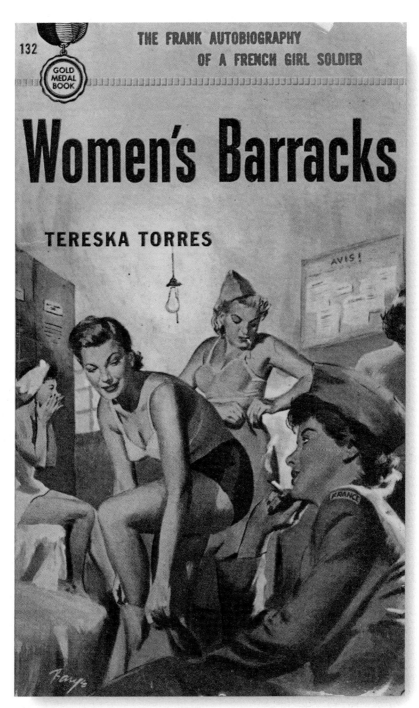

Gold Medal, 1950. Cover painting by Barye Phillips. The book that started all the excitement. A bestseller whose popularity was not hurt by its being named in a Senate investigation.

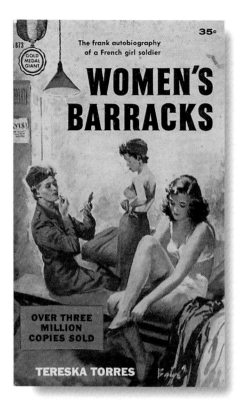

The frank autobiography of a French girl soldier

WOMEN'S BARRACKS

35¢

GOLD MEDAL GIANT

OVER THREE MILLION COPIES SOLD

TERESKA TORRES

Gold Medal, reprint. Cover painting by Barye Phillips. This new piece of art is slightly tamer than the original, keeping the lingerie but nixing the knowing stares between the two women in the foreground of the original.

> "... many of the scenes are as violent and depraved as any Faulkner has dealt with."—New Republic
>
> HOUSE OF FURY

Berkley, 1959. Cover painting by Robert Maguire. Reprint with sexy new art. The badder they are, the darker the hair.

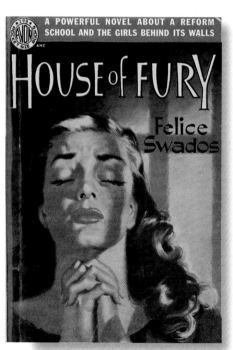

A POWERFUL NOVEL ABOUT A REFORM SCHOOL AND THE GIRLS BEHIND ITS WALLS

HOUSE of FURY
Felice Swados

Avon, 1950, reprint of a 1941 hardcover. Young, innocent girl corrupted by the system. A common, tragic plot device.

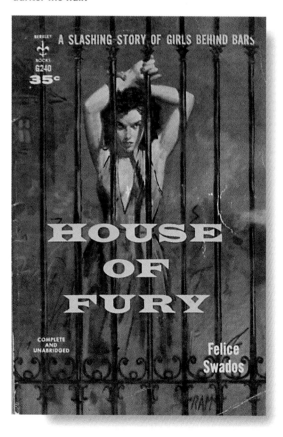

A SLASHING STORY OF GIRLS BEHIND BARS

BERKLEY BOOK
G-240
35¢

HOUSE OF FURY
Felice Swados

COMPLETE AND UNABRIDGED

Perma, 1953. Unusual cover art depicting older but still good-looking women.

Gold Medal, 1957. Cover painting by Barye Phillips. So innocent and vulnerable, just ripe for the picking.

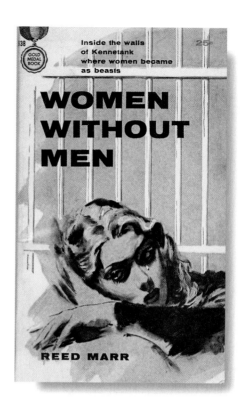

Inside the walls of Kennetank where women became as beasts

WOMEN WITHOUT MEN

REED MARR

A SHOCKING STORY OF LIVES AND FEMALE DESIRES WARPED BEYOND REASON BY A CRUEL AND SADISTIC IDEA OF JUSTICE

MIDWOOD
NO. 120

WOMEN IN PRISON

BY MIKE AVALLONE

Midwood, 1961. The sleaze cover art says it all.

"There are no men in a women's prison, but there is plenty of sex."
DEGRADED WOMEN

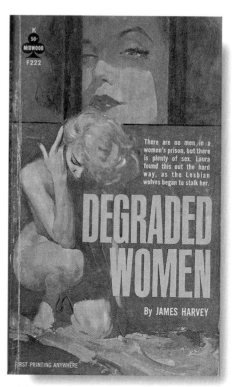

MIDWOOD
F222

There are no men in a women's prison, but there is plenty of sex. Laura found this out the hard way, as the Lesbian wolves began to stalk her.

DEGRADED WOMEN

By JAMES HARVEY

FIRST PRINTING ANYWHERE

Midwood, 1962. Cover painting by Robert Maguire.

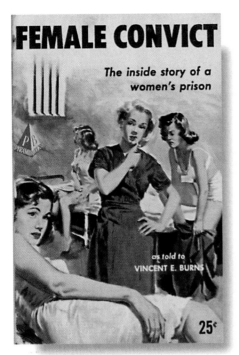

"A frank exposé of life behind bars... where lesbians took advantage of the terribly crowded quarters"

FEMALE CONVICT

Pyramid, 1952, reprint from an early hard-cover. Cover painting by Robert Maguire.

Pyramid, 1962. Cover painting by Robert Maguire. Life in a girls' reformatory. Scary, tough broads.

The inside story
of a women's prison

G373 35c

FEMALE CONVICT

as told to
VINCENT G. BURNS

Pyramid, 1959, reprint. Cover painting by Robert Maguire.

DEPRAVED WANTONS TRAPPED BY A WALL OF SIN!

REFORM SCHOOL GIRLS

By ANDREW SHAW

75¢
NB 1623

THIS IS AN ORIGINAL NIGHTSTAND BOOK

Nightstand, 1962. While most sleaze covers play up any lesbian angles, this one ignores it. Written by Lawrence Block as Andrew Shaw.

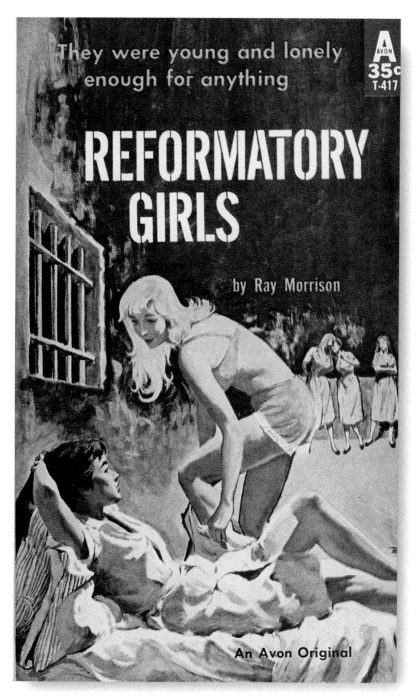

They were young and lonely enough for anything

REFORMATORY GIRLS

by Ray Morrison

An Avon Original

Avon, 1960. Cover painting by Darcy. A common scene on lesbian pulp fiction covers—a short-haired brunette butch with a long-haired blond femme. It's the girls in the background watching that's cool here.

A hundred women came to paradise
and a hundred angels fell

35¢

City of Women

NANCY MORGAN

AN ORIGINAL GIANT
BY GOLD MEDAL BOOKS

Red Seal, 1952. Cover painting by Barye Phillips. Women at war had the GIs, but they had each other too.

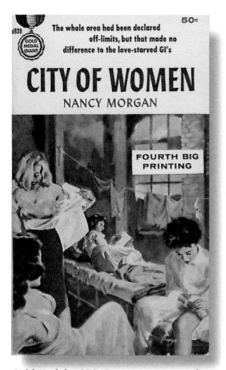

50¢

The whole area had been declared
off-limits, but that made no
difference to the love-starved GI's

CITY OF WOMEN
NANCY MORGAN

FOURTH BIG
PRINTING

Gold Medal, 1959. Same cover art as the
Red Seal, but with a more blatant selling
line.

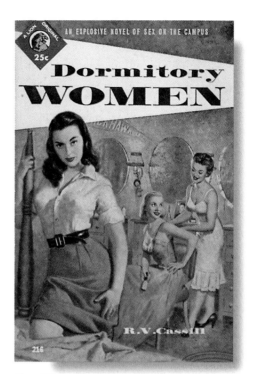

AN EXPLOSIVE NOVEL OF SEX ON THE CAMPUS

25¢

Dormitory
WOMEN

R.V. Cassill

216

Lion, 1955. This girl wants you!

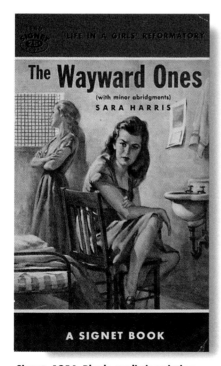

LIFE IN A GIRLS' REFORMATORY

The Wayward Ones
(with minor abridgments)
SARA HARRIS

A SIGNET BOOK

Signet, 1954. Bleak, realistic painting.

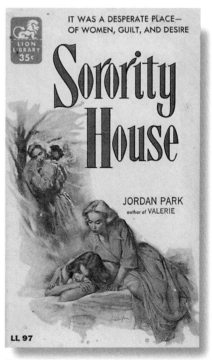

IT WAS A DESPERATE PLACE—
OF WOMEN, GUILT, AND DESIRE

LION
LIBRARY
35¢

Sorority
House

JORDAN PARK
author of VALERIE

LL 97

Lion, 1956. Cover painting by Clark Hulings.

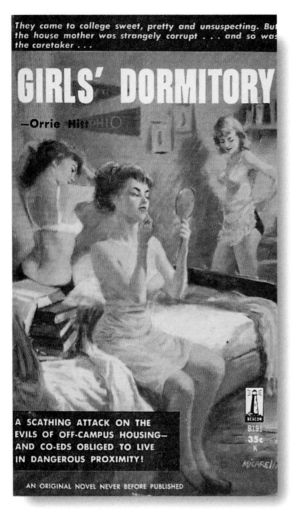

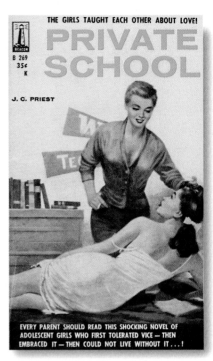

Beacon, 1959. Butchy redhead.

Beacon, 1958. Cover painting by Micarelli. Even with lots of undergarments, this is much less overt than *Private School* (above, right).

Midwood, 1963. Cover painting by Paul Rader. Pajamas never looked sexier! Penned by Ed Geis under the pseudonym Peggy Swenson.

Brandon House, 1964. Bobby socks and saddle shoes! Another Ed Geis book, with uncommon, wonderful line illustrations inside *(opposite, far right)*.

> "...She found herself
> a rival with her
> step-mother for
> the attention of a
> young girl..."
>
> INTO THE FIRE

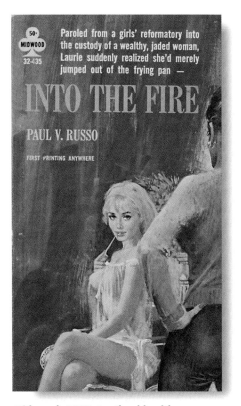

Midwood, 1965. Another blond femme.

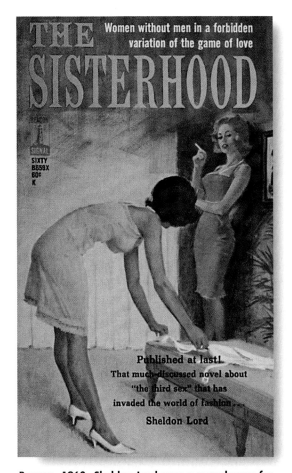

Beacon, 1963. Sheldon Lord was a pseudonym for
any of several writers, including Lawrence Block.

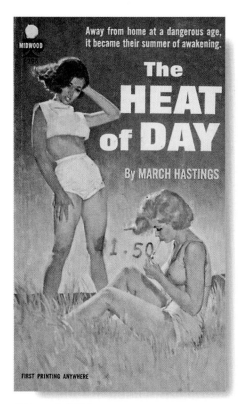

Away from home at a dangerous age, it became their summer of awakening.

The HEAT of DAY

By MARCH HASTINGS

1.50

FIRST PRINTING ANYWHERE

Midwood, 1963.

No one at school realized they were more than just roommates . . . no one suspected what took place once their door was locked.

50¢ MIDWOOD 32-479

PRIVATE PARTY

KIMBERLY KEMP

FIRST PRINTING ANYWHERE

Midwood, 1965.

Contrary to popular belief, *redheads* have more fun!

Every student majored in Sex and Vice at

SIN SCHOOL

By DON HOLLIDAY

AN ORIGINAL NOVEL

K 35¢

MIDWOOD

What The Students Learned In This School Of Hell

NO BOOK EVER TAUGHT!

Midwood, 1959.

CN/ PE 430/$1.25

THE OLIVE BRANCH

Leslie was a dedicated WAC, but she craved love enough to risk public humiliation to get it !

Pauline Cooper

Private Editions, 1967.

Positive Portraits

Spring Fire by Marijane Meaker as Vin Packer was the first paperback original to deal with a lesbian theme, and it opened up a whole new genre. While many later books were written by men, with little attention to authenticity, and were filled with stereotypical and misogynistic ideas about women and lesbians, this first novel and many other early ones published by Gold Medal did have the ring of truth about them because they were written by lesbians. Although they can be looked on as dated or quaint now, they still are readable and convey a sense of the time. Their popularity was based on the male readership, and so the covers were sexy and sensational. The books, however, were popular among lesbians also, and tattered copies were passed around in some circles. The depictions of women on the covers, and in the text, were possibly the only place a lesbian could find any image to identify with, no matter how inaccurate.

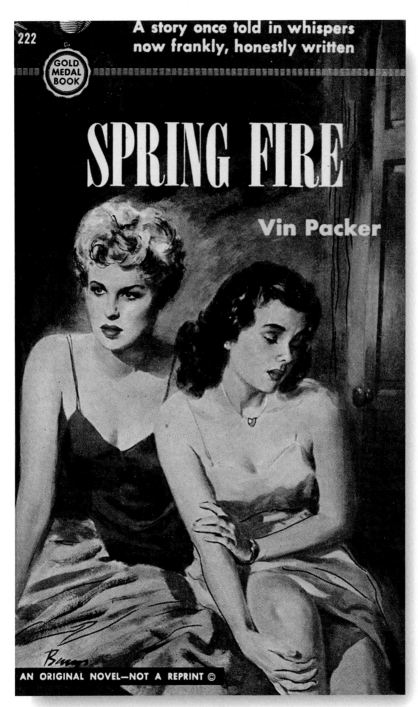

222

A story once told in whispers
now frankly, honestly written

GOLD
MEDAL
BOOK

SPRING FIRE

Vin Packer

AN ORIGINAL NOVEL—NOT A REPRINT ©

Gold Medal, 1952. Cover painting by Barye Phillips. The first Gold Medal original with a lesbian theme. Its immediate success started a whole new subgenre of original fiction. Marijane Meaker, who wrote as Vin Packer and Ann Aldrich, is still writing gay/lesbian young adult fiction as M. E. Kerr.

Gold Medal, 1958. A cheap way to have a new cover treatment was to reuse the art with different type.

> "Lesbian is an ugly word and I hate it. But that's what I am."
>
> SPRING FIRE

Gold Medal, 1957. Cover painting by Barye Phillips. Ann Bannon's first novel, a very accurate portrayal, but the man gets the girl in the end.

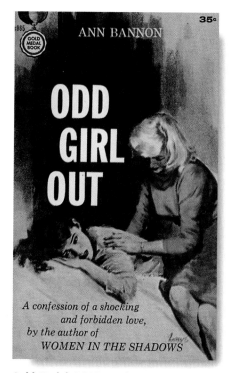

Gold Medal, 1960, reprint. Cover painting by Barye Phillips. The same pose but slightly more realistic than the first edition.

Crest, 1957. The photo cover makes this look a little sleazy, but it is a well-written and sensitive portrait of lesbian life in the 1950s. A blurb in the front asks parents to read this book and take responsibility for their "immature boys and girls."

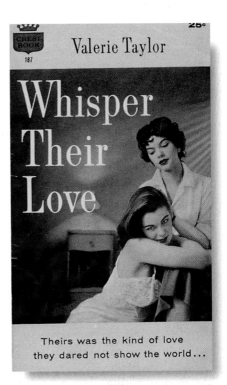

Crest, 1958. The quote from *The New York Times* on the front gives the novel a slight legitimacy that the cover art belies.

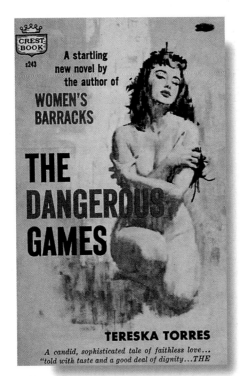

Crest, 1961. Reprint with sultry new cover art and a quote from Ann Aldrich.

Of the love that dwells in twilight
—the "love that can never be told"

WE WALK
ALONE
Through Lesbos' Lonely Groves

GOLD
MEDAL
BOOK

$774

35¢

ANN ALDRICH

Gold Medal, 1958. It's amazing how far a little classical allusion lets the cover art go in terms of nudity. Written by Marijane Meaker as Ann Aldrich.

35¢

27

GOLD MEDAL GIANT

ANN ALDRICH
Author of the controversial WE WALK ALONE

We, too, must love

"An honest book, a book necessary to light up the dark places of our society."

—DR. RICHARD S. HOFFMANN
WORLD-FAMOUS PSYCHIATRIST

Gold Medal, 1958. Another well-written, positive look at lesbian life, this was a followup to *We Walk Alone.*

"'They wanted to know if I knew what 'gay' meant. I said sure— happy, fun, jolly.'"

WE, TOO, MUST LOVE

d1009

GOLD MEDAL GIANT

50¢

CAROL
IN A
THOUSAND CITIES

The twilight woman— as she sees herself, and as she is seen through the eyes of others, including

SIMONE de BEAUVOIR
SIGMUND FREUD
CLAIRE MORGAN
GUY de MAUPASSANT
FRANCOISE MALLET
and others

edited by
ANN ALDRICH

Gold Medal, 1960. Short story collection.

AN INTIMATE PICTURE OF WOMEN IN LOVE
---WITH EACH OTHER!

THREE WOMEN

March Hastings

B 190
35¢
K

'Tender, yet deeply revealing.... A courageous
excursion into a forbidden world.'

Beacon, 1958. Homosexuality in Manhattan
art circles.

"Val sensed something oddly
disturbing about the girl. Not
until later did she realize what
it was—and then it was much
too late!"
EDGE OF TWILIGHT

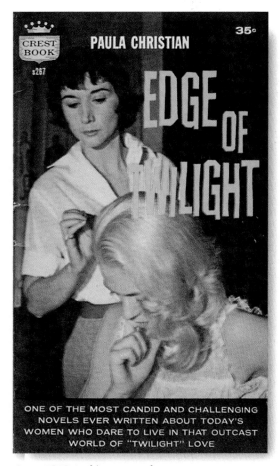

CREST BOOK
$267

PAULA CHRISTIAN
35¢

EDGE OF TWILIGHT

ONE OF THE MOST CANDID AND CHALLENGING
NOVELS EVER WRITTEN ABOUT TODAY'S
WOMEN WHO DARE TO LIVE IN THAT OUTCAST
WORLD OF "TWILIGHT" LOVE

Crest, 1959. Lesbian stewardesses.

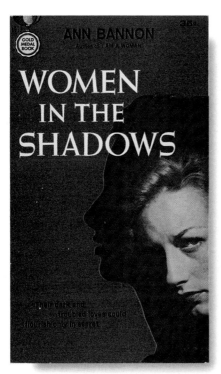

Gold Medal, 1959. Predatory lesbians.

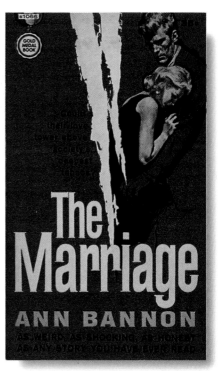

Gold Medal, 1960. Nice vignette art.

Gold Medal, 1960.

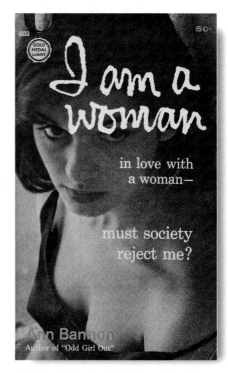

Gold Medal, 1959. Look at that cleavage!

GOLD
MEDAL
d1224

50¢

GAY ST.

ONE WAY

ONE WAY

Lost, lonely,
boyishly
appealing—
this is

Beebo Brinker

—who never
really knew what
she wanted—
until she came
to Greenwich
Village and
found the love
that smoulders
in the shadows of
the twilight world

A NOVEL BY ANN BANNON
AUTHOR OF I AM A WOMAN AND ODD GIRL OUT

Gold Medal, 1962. Cover painting by Robert McGinnis. He obviously had no idea
what a butch looked like.

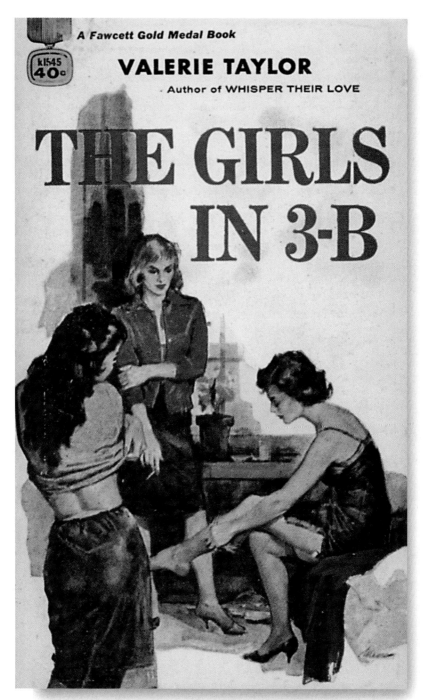

A Fawcett Gold Medal Book

VALERIE TAYLOR

Author of WHISPER THEIR LOVE

THE GIRLS IN 3-B

k1545
40¢

Gold Medal, 1959. This is what happens in Greenwich Village.

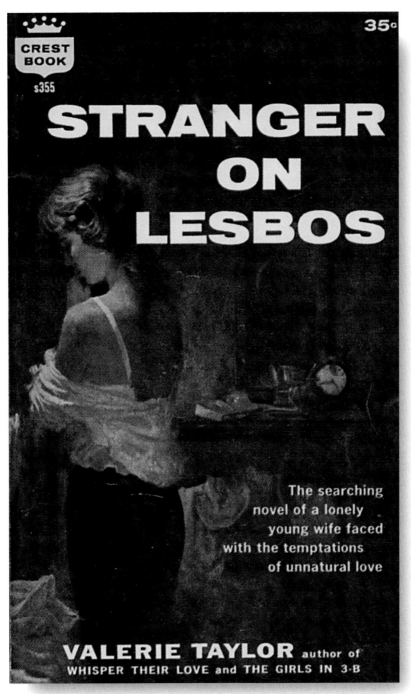

CREST BOOK

s355

35c

STRANGER ON LESBOS

The searching
novel of a lonely
young wife faced
with the temptations
of unnatural love

VALERIE TAYLOR author of
WHISPER THEIR LOVE and THE GIRLS IN 3-B

Crest, 1960. A moody portrait.

418

MONARCH BOOKS 40¢

They Lived And Loved In The Off-Beat
World Of Lesbianism

TWILIGHT LOVERS

Miriam Gardner
First Publication Anywhere

Monarch, 1964. Cover painting by Rafael M. DeSoto. Once again, the butch
has short, dark hair, although she's wearing a femmy brassiere and capri
pants, and the femme has longish blond hair. Written by Marion Zimmer
Bradley as Miriam Gardner.

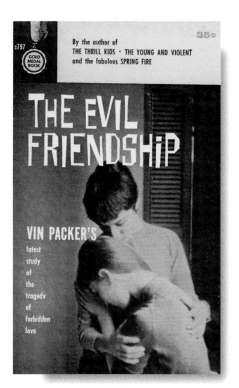

By the author of
THE THRILL KIDS · THE YOUNG AND VIOLENT
and the fabulous SPRING FIRE

35¢

#797

GOLD MEDAL BOOK

THE EVIL FRIENDSHIP

VIN PACKER'S

latest
study
of
the
tragedy
of
forbidden
love

Gold Medal, 1958. Despite the exploitational title, the cover photo is quite sensitive. The story is a fictionalized account of the infamous New Zealand Parker-Hulme trial, called the "female Leopold-Loeb case," which was also made into a 1995 film, *Heavenly Creatures.* Interestingly enough, one of the accused girls, now an adult, writes mysteries as Anne Perry.

"Then hungrily they fed on each other's lips. Martha grasped Mary Drew's hand. 'Love me, will you? Not just kisses. Not any more.'"

THE EVIL FRIENDSHIP

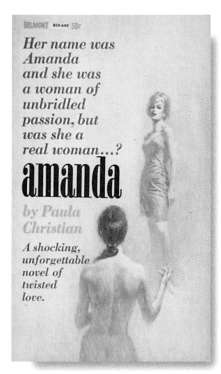

BELMONT 850-640 50¢

Her name was
Amanda
and she was
a woman of
unbridled
passion, but
was she a
real woman...?

amanda

by Paula
Christian

A shocking,
unforgettable
novel of
twisted
love.

Belmont, 1965.

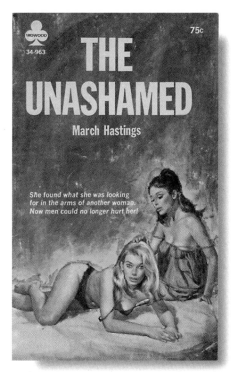

MIDWOOD 75¢
34-963

THE UNASHAMED

March Hastings

She found what she was looking for in the arms of another woman. Now men could no longer hurt her!

Midwood, 1968. Cover painting by Paul Rader. Sexy package for a sensitive book.

Strange Sisters

Strange \'stranj\ *adj* **strang•er; strang•est** [ME, fr. OF *estrange,* fr. L *extraneus,* lit., external, fr. *extra* outside—more at EXTRA-] (13c) **1 a** *archaic* : of, relating to, or characteristic of another country : FOREIGN **b** : not native to or naturally belonging in a place : of external origin, kind, or character **2 a** : not before known, heard, or seen : UNFAMILIAR **b** : exciting wonder or awe : EXTRAORDINARY **3 a** : discouraging familiarities : RESERVED, DISTANT **b** : ILL AT EASE **4** : UNACCUSTOMED TO <she was ~ to his ways> **5** : having the quantum characteristic of strangeness <~ quark> <~ particle> — **strange•ly** *adv* **/ syn** STRANGE, SINGULAR, UNIQUE, PECULIAR, ECCENTRIC, ERRATIC, ODD, QUEER, QUAINT, OUT-LANDISH mean departing from what is ordinary, usual, or to be expected . . .

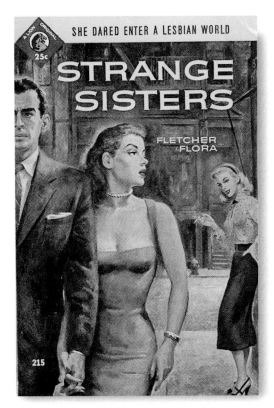

"The slender bookshelf of outstanding works about sexual deviations must now make room for Fletcher Flora's honest and perceptive novel, Strange Sisters."

STRANGE SISTERS

Lion, 1954.

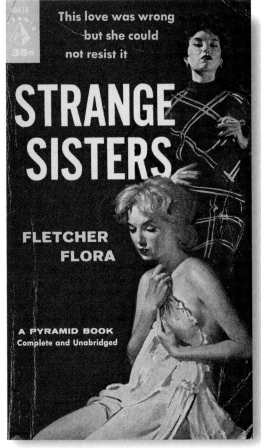

Pyramid, 1960. Cover painting by Robert Maguire.

A RAGING TORRENT OF MIXED EMOTIONS...

STRANGE PASSIONS

By **Florence Stonebraker**

AN
ORIGINAL NOVEL
Not a Reprint

...A Whispered-About
Subject !

Safran

Croydon, 1953. Cover painting by Bernard Safran. An artist and her model.

Theirs was a love that defied society

A PYRAMID GIANT
35c
G170

STRANGE FRIENDS

AGNETE HOLK

Pyramid Giant, 1955. Translated from Danish. Smoking seems to be a butch thing, a manifestation of penis envy, no doubt.

PYRAMID BOOKS R-863 50c

THE UNSPOKEN SECRET OF A TWILIGHT LOVE

STRANGE FRIENDS

AGNETE HOLK

Pyramid, 1963, reprint. Cover painting by Ronnie Lesser à la Maguire.

"This novel is the story of the almost unspeakable revenge sought by a man who lost his woman...to another woman."

STRANGE SEDUCTION

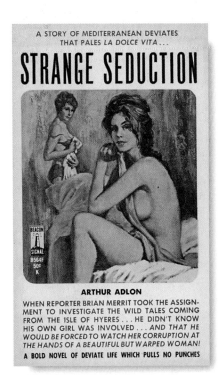

A STORY OF MEDITERRANEAN DEVIATES
THAT PALES *LA DOLCE VITA*...

STRANGE SEDUCTION

BEACON SIGNAL
B564F 50c
K

ARTHUR ADLON

WHEN REPORTER BRIAN MERRIT TOOK THE ASSIGN-MENT TO INVESTIGATE THE WILD TALES COMING FROM THE ISLE OF HYERES...HE DIDN'T KNOW HIS OWN GIRL WAS INVOLVED...AND THAT HE WOULD BE FORCED TO WATCH HER CORRUPTION AT THE HANDS OF A BEAUTIFUL BUT WARPED WOMAN!

A BOLD NOVEL OF DEVIATE LIFE WHICH PULLS NO PUNCHES

Beacon, 1962. Cover painting by Victor Olsen.

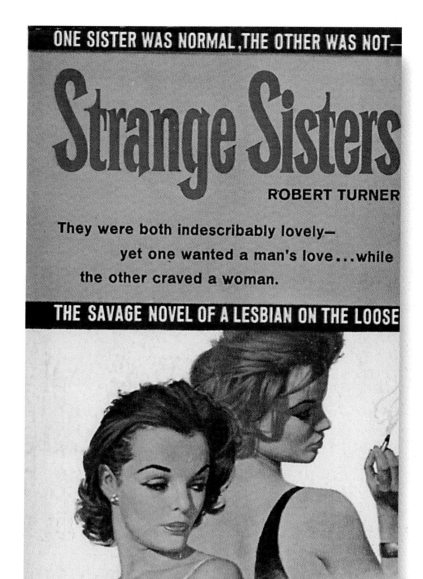

ONE SISTER WAS NORMAL, THE OTHER WAS NOT—

Strange Sisters

ROBERT TURNER

They were both indescribably lovely—
yet one wanted a man's love...while
the other craved a woman.

THE SAVAGE NOVEL OF A LESBIAN ON THE LOOSE

B526F 50¢ K

Beacon, 1962. Savage!

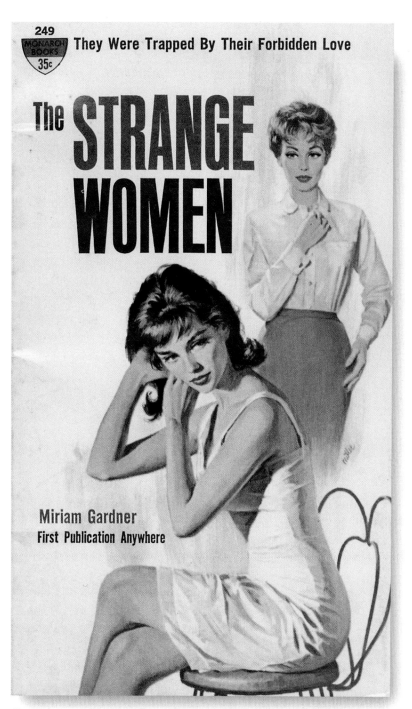

249

MONARCH BOOKS

35¢

They Were Trapped By Their Forbidden Love

The STRANGE WOMEN

Miriam Gardner
First Publication Anywhere

Monarch, 1962. Cover painting by Tom Miller. Written by Marion Zimmer Bradley as Miriam Gardner. The brunette in the slip is the femme, and the red-headed butch wears the plain mannish shirt.

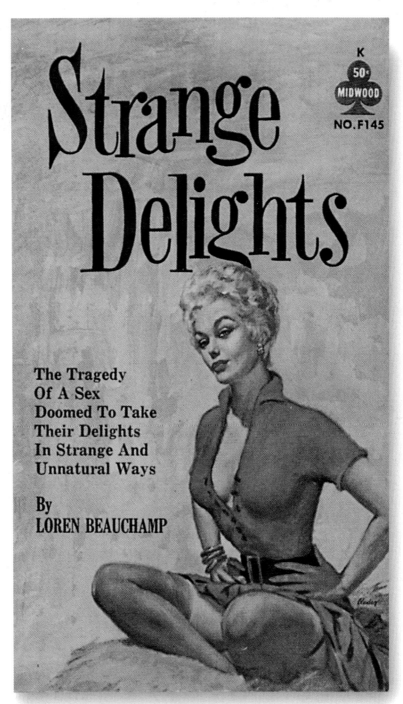

Midwood, 1962. Cover painting by Paul Rader. Written by Robert Silverberg as Loren Beauchamp, with one of the sexiest covers in my collection.

THE STRANGE TRIO

FLAME

FB-106
95¢

Three girls who could not resist the forbidden fruit of their special kind of love.

RHONA ROLLINS

FOR ADULT READING

Flame, 1967. Cover painting by Robert Maguire. His women always have beautiful eyes!

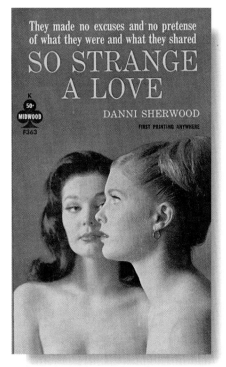

They made no excuses and no pretense of what they were and what they shared

SO STRANGE A LOVE

DANNI SHERWOOD

K
50¢
MIDWOOD
F363

FIRST PRINTING ANYWHERE

Midwood, 1964. Amazing photo cover.

STRANGE THIRSTS

The Setting
a famous university campus
The Scene
the annual college play
The Star
a renowned actress whose warped desires embrace men and women alike

K
60¢
B662X
BEACON

SIGNAL
SIXTY

Michael Norday

Beacon Signal, 1963. Bisexual campus fun.

""Is this the first time for you?
...Don't be afraid...
I'll teach you everything.'"

STRANGE THIRSTS

Cliterature

Although the covers are no different, the quality of the writing and the intent of the author separate these novels from the paperback originals. First published in hardcover, to mostly favorable reviews, these books are still quite readable and give an authenic and sympathetic potrait of lesbian life in their times. The books that were printed in the thirties are the most remarkable, including Radclyffe Hall's *The Well of Loneliness*. Banned in England upon publication in 1928, it was reprinted in the 1950s by Perma Books. It is the grandmother of all lesbian-themed books and still remains in print, some seventy years after it was first written.

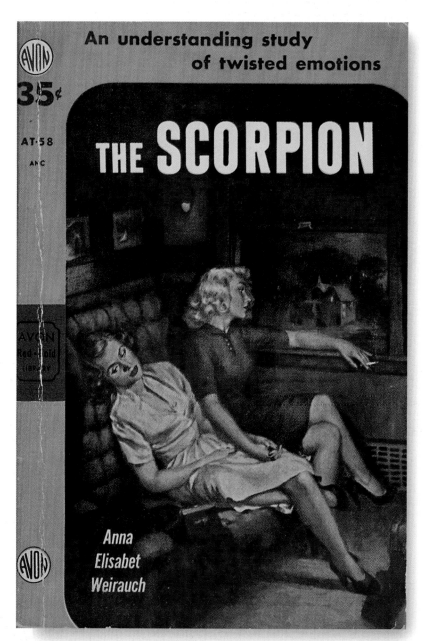

Avon, 1948. Written by Anna Elisabet Weirauch. Reprinted from the German hardcover edition, 1932.

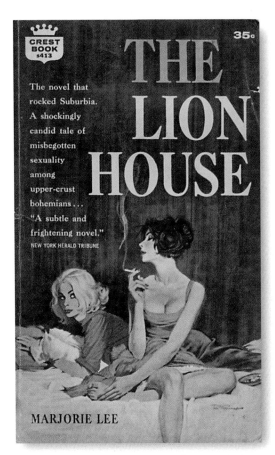

Crest, 1960. Cover painting by Robert McGinnis.

"Together they cling and together they struggle for understanding in an unsympathetic world."

THE SCORPION

Bantam, 1951. Reprinted from the French hardcover edition, 1949.

1148

BANTAM BOOKS

25¢

THE NOVEL OF A LOVE SOCIETY FORBIDS

THE PRICE OF SALT

CLAIRE MORGAN

"[handles] explosive material...
with sincerity and good taste." New York Times

Bantam, 1953. Cover painting by Barye Phillips. Written by Patricia Highsmith as Claire Morgan. The art is full of angst, with harsh angles and exaggerated shadows. Note the tormented former boyfriend in the background, although the girls hardly seem to.

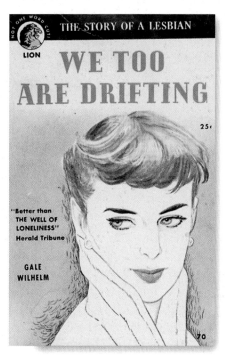

THE STORY OF A LESBIAN

WE TOO ARE DRIFTING

25¢

"Better than THE WELL OF LONELINESS" Herald Tribune

GALE WILHELM

Lion, 1951. First published in 1935, a wonderfully literate book that's still in print.

a one-time LESBIAN tells her strange story

either is LOVE

elisabeth craigin

25¢

Lion, 1952. First published in 1937. Sensitive and nonconfrontational.

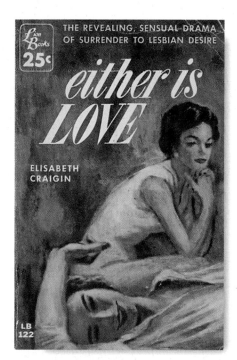

THE REVEALING, SENSUAL DRAMA OF SURRENDER TO LESBIAN DESIRE

25¢

either is LOVE

ELISABETH CRAIGIN

Lion, 1956. Cover painting by David Stone. Very subtle, and only slightly more daring than the 1952 edition (*above*).

G497

35¢

The revealing, sensual drama of surrender to strange desire

either is LOVE

ELISABETH CRAIGIN

"Not told sensationally .. sophisticated and intelligent." —NEW YORK TIMES

Pyramid, 1960. Cover painting by Tom Miller.

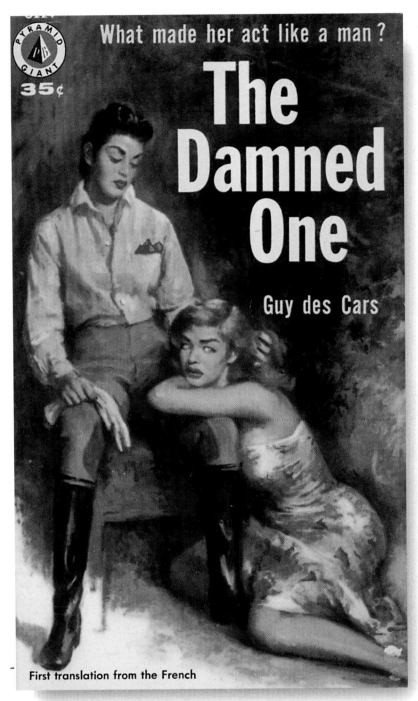

What made her act like a man?

The Damned One

Guy des Cars

PYRAMID GIANT

35¢

First translation from the French

Pyramid, 1956. Cover painting by George Ziel. Reprinted from the French hard-cover. The butch with open-collared shirt, riding pants and boots makes this painting one of the hottest and most risqué, despite the lack of nudity.

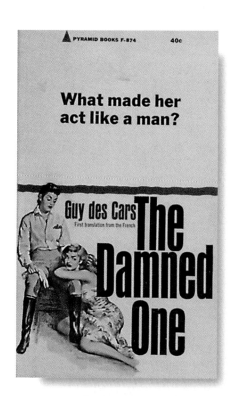

Pyramid, 1963, reprint. Cover painting by George Ziel. The selling line is highlighted, and the art is almost a second thought, which is too bad.

"'Claude!' She panted. 'You kiss me like a man.'"

THE DAMNED ONE

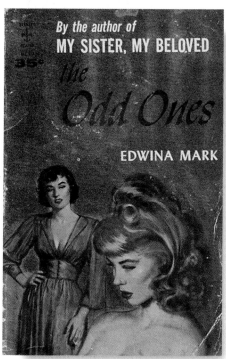

Berkley, 1959. Cover painting by Rudolph Nappi. Written by Edwin Fadiman, Jr., as Edwina Mark.

Berkley, ND. Reprinted from a 1939 hardcover autobiography that had a subtitle, "A Strange Autobiography."

Psycho-Babble

While the Kinsey Report brought a wider understanding of sexuality to middle America, it was still the 1950s of Eisenhower, McCarthy and suburban dreams. The Select Committee on Current Pornographic Materials was appointed and the threat of censorship was on publishers' minds. However, a loophole was found! A book could not be censored if it was, or could pretend to be, a serious scientific study. Thus, all sorts of "scientific" studies of sexuality and deviant sexuality were printed. Couched in medical terminology, with introductions and testimonials by alleged psychiatrists and M.D.s, these books were doused in legitimacy, and often offered more risqué reading material than the novels.

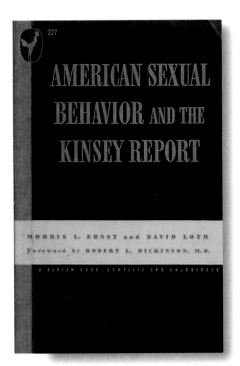

Bantam, 1948. Kinsey made reading about sex almost legitimate—it was science.

Dell First Edition, 1953. Cover painting by Walter Brooks. Very "scientific," with an introduction by sociologist Margaret Mead.

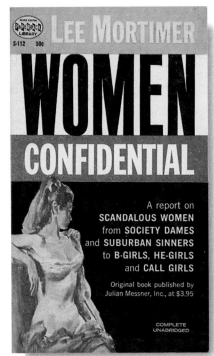

Paperback Library, 1961. ". . . final word on women going to hell from suburbia to Shanghai. . . ."

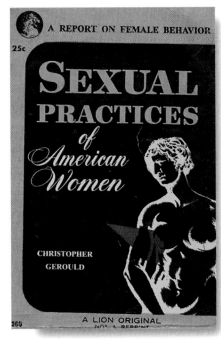

Lion, 1953. What does the red triangle jutting out of her breast mean?

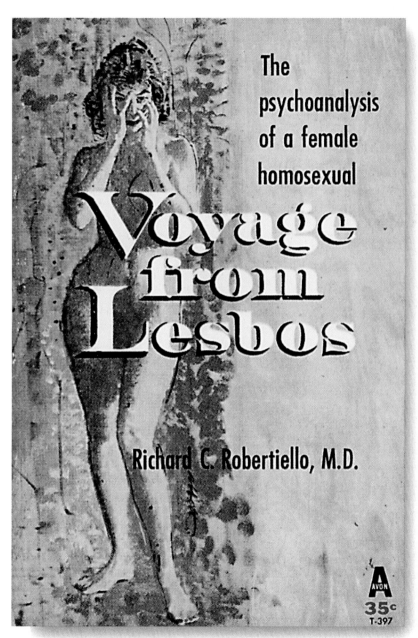

The
psychoanalysis
of a female
homosexual

Voyage from Lesbos

Richard C. Robertiello, M.D.

AVON 35¢ T-397

Avon, 1959. The shame of it all.

A Problem That Must Be Faced!

THE LESBIAN IN OUR SOCIETY

By W. D. SPRAGUE, Ph. D.

DETAILED CASE HISTORIES OF THE THIRD SEX

K
50¢
MIDWOOD
NO. F154

Midwood, 1962. The book that started my obsession.

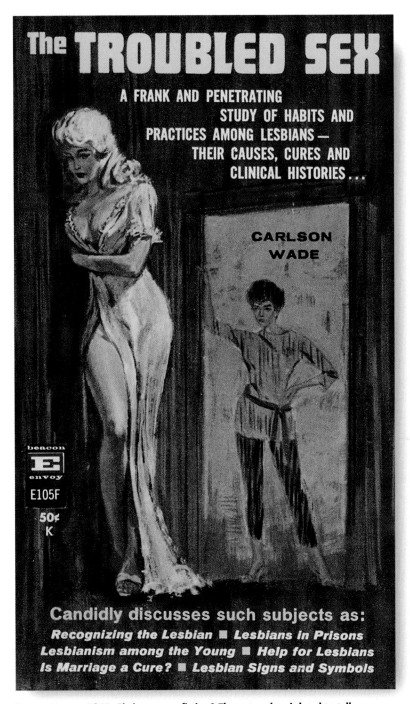

Beacon Envoy, 1961. Fiction or nonfiction? The art makes it hard to tell.

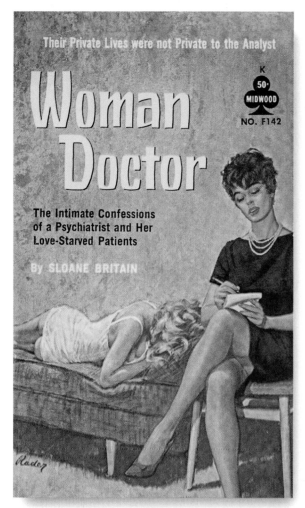

Their Private Lives were not Private to the Analyst

Woman Doctor

K
50¢
MIDWOOD
NO. F142

The Intimate Confessions
of a Psychiatrist and Her
Love-Starved Patients

By SLOANE BRITAIN

Midwood, 1962. Cover painting by Paul Rader. He gives us breast cleavage and rear cleavage in the same pose!

"She bent her head closer to Mavis and kissed her. Pleasure flashed through her like a sanctifying sword."
WOMAN DOCTOR

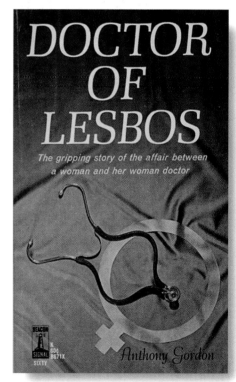

DOCTOR OF LESBOS

The gripping story of the affair between a woman and her woman doctor

BEACON
SIGNAL
SIXTY

Anthony Gordon

Beacon, 1963. Same concept as *Woman Doctor,* but with an exceptionally restrained cover.

"More personal than the Kinsey Report..."

SEX HABITS OF SINGLE WOMEN

LILLIAN PRESTON

This bold new book is an encyclopedia of the sexual practices and erotic fantasies of modern unmarried women. *With case histories in their own words...*

Beacon, 1964. Cover vignette by Robert Maguire. Interviews with lesbians!

Dangerous Desires

Every cliché and stereotype about lesbianism and homosexuality was exploited by publishers to attract readers. Frigidity, nymphomania, promiscuity, bisexuality, predatory dispositions! Lesbianism was linked to everything dark and evil—sadism and masochism, bondage and discipline, satanism and witchcraft—even murder.

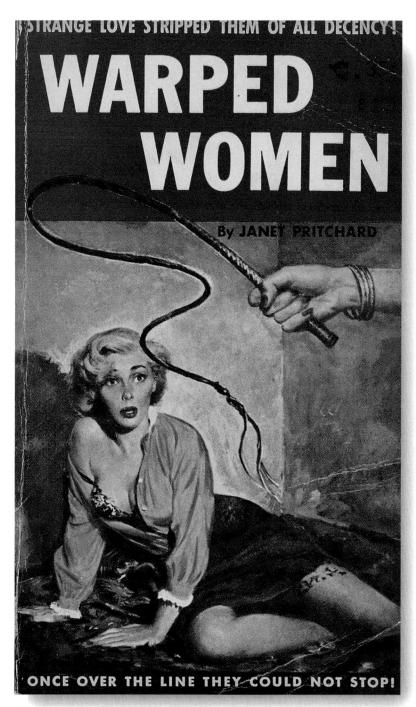

Beacon, 1951. Lesbianism and sadism.

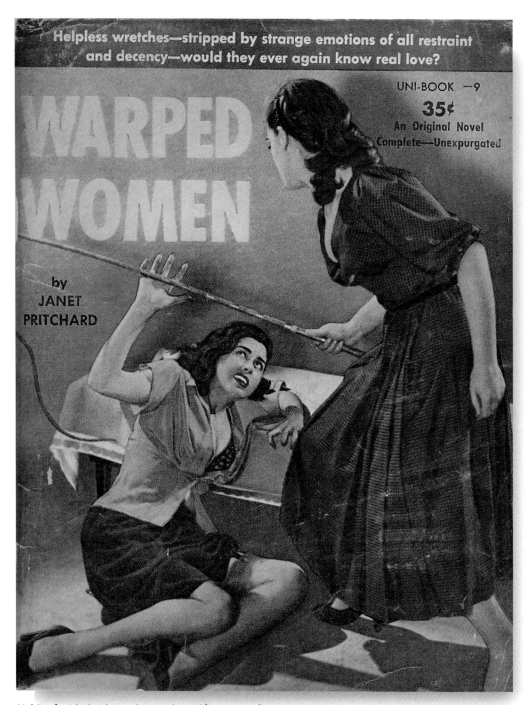

Helpless wretches—stripped by strange emotions of all restraint and decency—would they ever again know real love?

UNI-BOOK —9

35¢

An Original Novel
Complete—Unexpurgated

WARPED WOMEN

by
JANET
PRITCHARD

Uni-Book, 1953. Digest-size version with a camp photo cover.

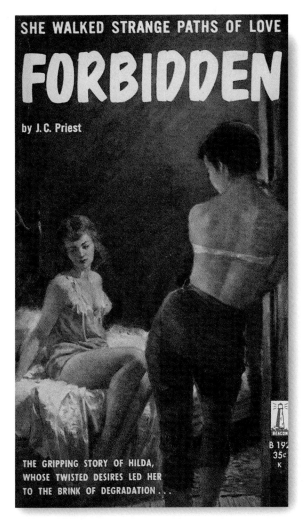

SHE WALKED STRANGE PATHS OF LOVE

FORBIDDEN

by J.C. Priest

THE GRIPPING STORY OF HILDA, WHOSE TWISTED DESIRES LED HER TO THE BRINK OF DEGRADATION . . .

BEACON

B 192
35¢
K

Beacon, 1952.

"Was I a lesbian? Was I?
I honestly didn't know and
when it came right down
to questions of sex I was
frightfully confused."

WARPED DESIRE

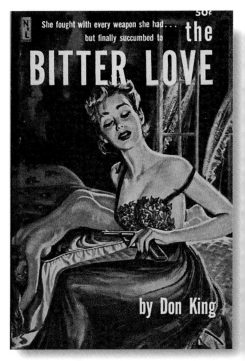

She fought with every weapon she had . . .
but finally succumbed to

the

BITTER LOVE

by Don King

50¢

Newsstand Library, 1959. Lesbianism leads to death . . .

94

...BOLDLY PROBES
THE PROBLEM OF THE
FRIGID WOMAN,
FORCED BY HER OWN
DESPERATION INTO
UNNATURAL PATHS!

warped
DESIRE

B-289
35¢
K

Kay Addams

Beacon, 1960. Frigidity leads to lesbianism.

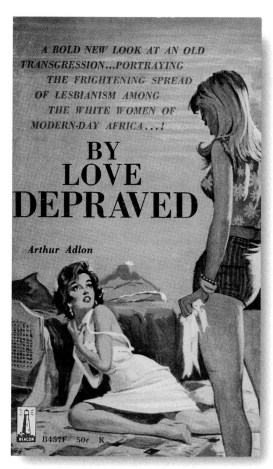

A BOLD NEW LOOK AT AN OLD
TRANSGRESSION...PORTRAYING
THE FRIGHTENING SPREAD
OF LESBIANISM AMONG
THE WHITE WOMEN OF
MODERN-DAY AFRICA...!

BY
LOVE
DEPRAVED

Arthur Adlon

BEACON B457F 50¢ K

Beacon, 1961. Cover painting by Darcy.

"'. . . you've got to start
acting like a gay girl,
Sheila. You won't be able
to lead a normal life any-
more, honey. Not now."
OF SHAME AND JOY

OF
SHAME AND
JOY

Women In Love—
But Not With Men

by SHELDON LORD
(an original novel)

•50•
MIDWOOD
NO. F121

A Compelling Novel Of Strange And Twisted Desires

Midwood, 1961. Cover painting by Paul Rader.
Lesbianism and nymphomania.

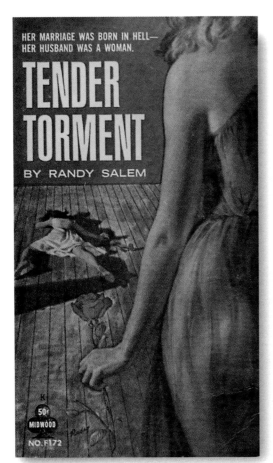

HER MARRIAGE WAS BORN IN HELL—
HER HUSBAND WAS A WOMAN.

TENDER TORMENT

BY RANDY SALEM

K
50¢
MIDWOOD
NO. F172

Midwood, 1962. Cover painting by Paul Rader.
Dead lesbians.

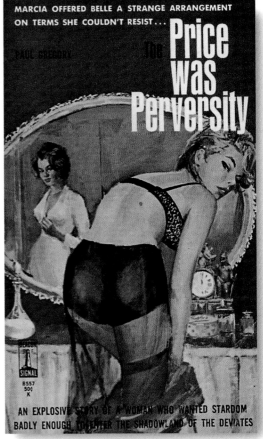

MARCIA OFFERED BELLE A STRANGE ARRANGEMENT
ON TERMS SHE COULDN'T RESIST...

PAUL GREGORY

The Price was Perversity

SIGNAL
B557
50¢
K

AN EXPLOSIVE STORY OF A WOMAN WHO WANTED STARDOM
BADLY ENOUGH TO ENTER THE SHADOWLAND OF THE DEVIATES

Beacon, 1962. Lesbians as ruthless predators.

"A penetrating Novel
that Reveals Why and
How some women
embrace abnormal love"
THE PRICE WAS PERVERSITY

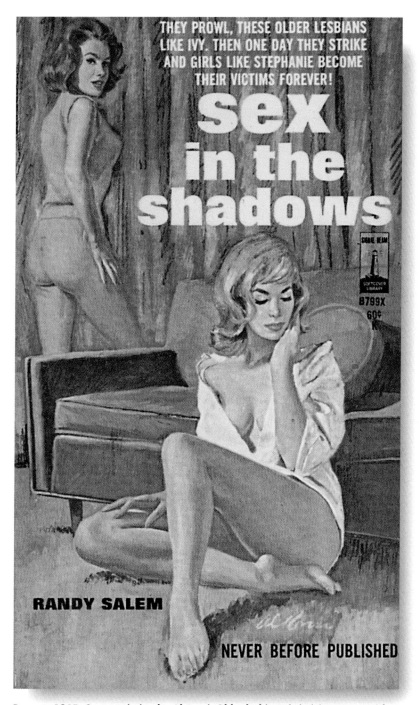

THEY PROWL, THESE OLDER LESBIANS LIKE IVY. THEN ONE DAY THEY STRIKE AND GIRLS LIKE STEPHANIE BECOME THEIR VICTIMS FOREVER!

sex in the shadows

8799X
60¢

RANDY SALEM

NEVER BEFORE PUBLISHED

Beacon, 1965. Cover painting by Al Rossi. Older lesbian victimizing young girls.

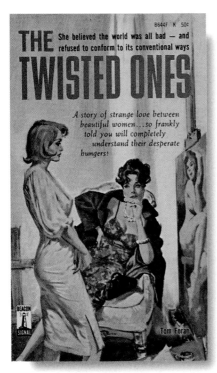

Beacon, 1963. Lesbians in the art world.

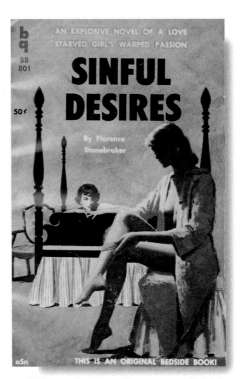

Bedside Book, ND. "Strange Passions ... Forbidden Lusts."

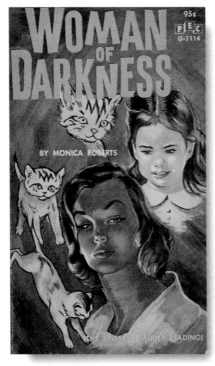

PEC, 1966. Lesbianism and witchcraft!

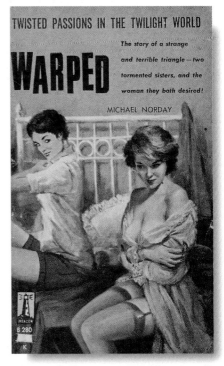

Beacon, 1963. Cover painting by Micarelli.

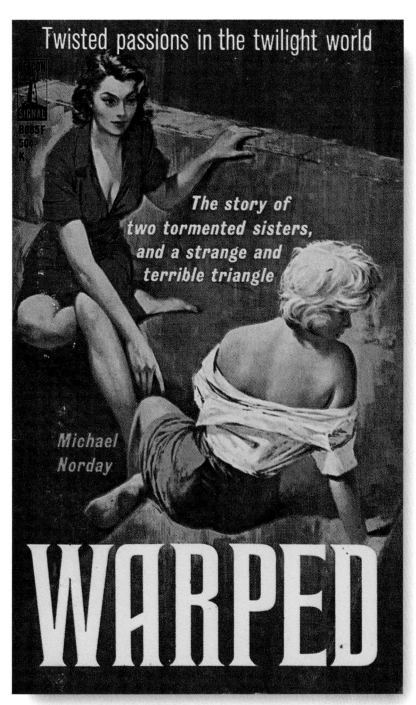

Beacon, 1955. Promiscuous lesbians.

Longing Looks

Is she or isn't she? Just follow her gaze. The best cover artists captured a wide range of emotions on canvas and conveyed them through the eyes: unrequited love, innocence lost, coy flirtations, outright lust, ecstasy. Many drew the women staring out from the covers directly at the reader, making a powerful plea for attention. Other covers may be more titillating and overtly sexual, but these covers convey an emotional connection that can be intimate and startling.

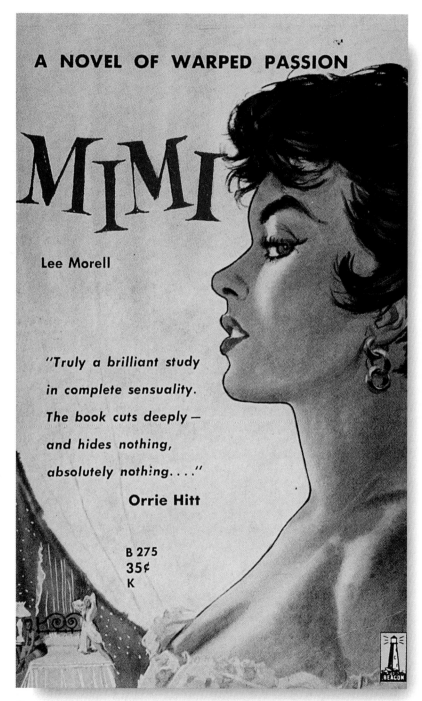

A NOVEL OF WARPED PASSION

MIMI

Lee Morell

"Truly a brilliant study in complete sensuality. The book cuts deeply — and hides nothing, absolutely nothing...."

Orrie Hitt

B 275
35¢
K

Beacon, 1959. What a look. Notice the small inset of the two girls on the bed.

Beacon, 1959.

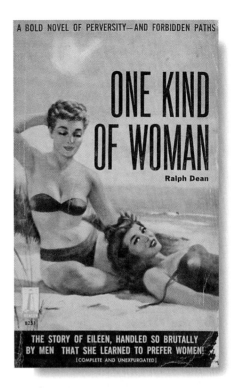

A BOLD NOVEL OF PERVERSITY—AND FORBIDDEN PATHS

ONE KIND OF WOMAN

Ralph Dean

THE STORY OF EILEEN, HANDLED SO BRUTALLY
BY MEN THAT SHE LEARNED TO PREFER WOMEN!
[COMPLETE AND UNEXPURGATED]

50¢

First person
3rd sex

The world of the les...the furtive
cult of strange loves and fierce passions.
by Sloane Britain

Newsstand Library, 1959. Smoldering.

"'Just relax, darling.
Just close your eyes and
pretend I'm a man.'"
ONE KIND OF WOMAN

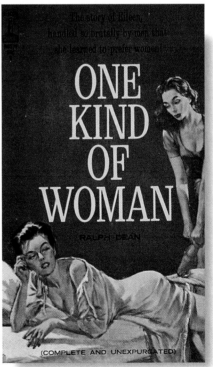

The story of Eileen,
handled so brutally by men that
she learned to prefer women!

ONE
KIND
OF
WOMAN

RALPH DEAN

(COMPLETE AND UNEXPURGATED)

Beacon Signal, 1963, 2nd edition.

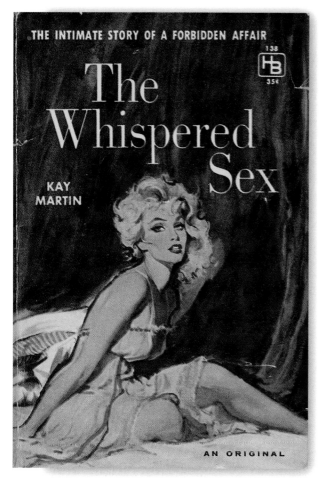

THE INTIMATE STORY OF A FORBIDDEN AFFAIR

The
Whispered
Sex

KAY
MARTIN

AN ORIGINAL

Hillman, 1960. Cover painting by Darcy.

"She had come in from the pool naked and Joyce found herself looking at the aesthetically proportioned body, then turning away, unaccountably embarrassed."

THE WHISPERED SEX

CAN A CALL GIRL
REALLY ENJOY LOVE
THE WAY OTHER WOMEN DO?

the
Sisters
Norman Bligh

A frank
portrait of
two girls in the
world's oldest
profession — and
an intimate
picture of
the sensual life
they shared!

B363
35¢
K

Beacon, 1960. A very risqué cover, with almost full nudity.

106

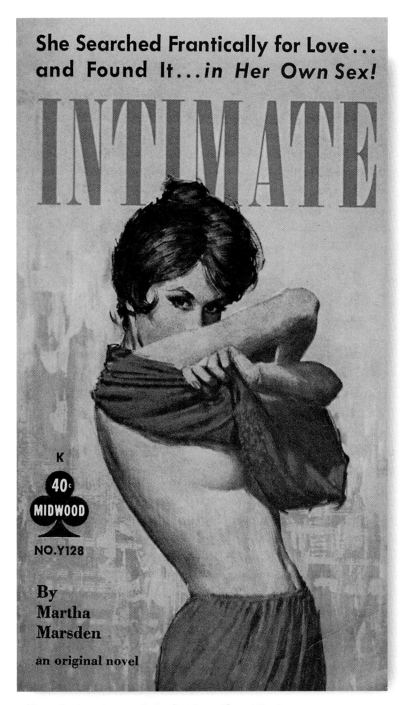

Midwood, 1961. Cover painting by Victor Olsen. Wow!

Midwood, 1961. Cover painting by Paul Rader. Proving backs can be sexy as well.

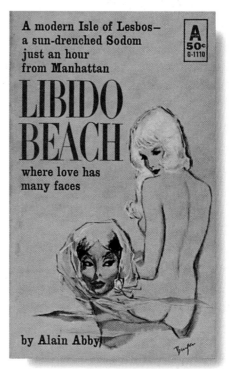

Avon, 1962. Cover painting by Barye Phillips. Unusual minimalist style.

"It began with a kiss.
A kiss hot as a blowtorch .."

HER WOMAN

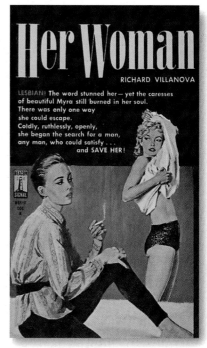

Beacon, 1962. Again, brunette butches and blond femmes.

Beacon, 1963.

Midwood, 1962. Cover painting by Paul Rader. There is actually a Gay Street in New York's Greenwich Village.

"Two call girls who played for pay, but when they played for keeps they played with each other"

VOLUPTUOUS VOYAGE

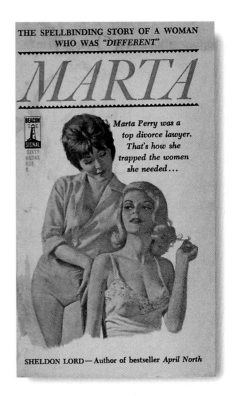

THE SPELLBINDING STORY OF A WOMAN WHO WAS "DIFFERENT"

MARTA

Marta Perry was a top divorce lawyer. That's how she trapped the women she needed...

SHELDON LORD — Author of bestseller *April North*

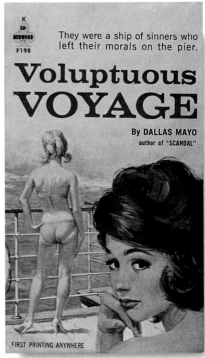

They were a ship of sinners who left their morals on the pier.

Voluptuous VOYAGE

By DALLAS MAYO
author of "SCANDAL"

FIRST PRINTING ANYWHERE

Midwood, 1962. Lesbians on the high seas.

Beacon, 1962. Cover painting by Darcy. Lesbians in the fashion world.

> "Haze knew two kinds of sex: what you had to do with men—and the kind you enjoyed if you found the right girl."
>
> THE ODD KIND

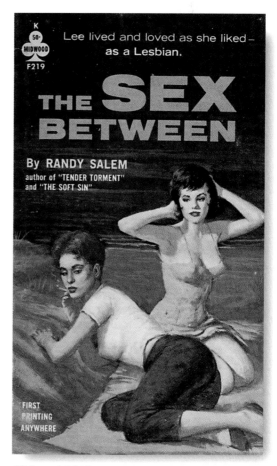

Midwood, 1962.

Monarch, 1963. Cover painting by Robert Maguire. . . . So do I.

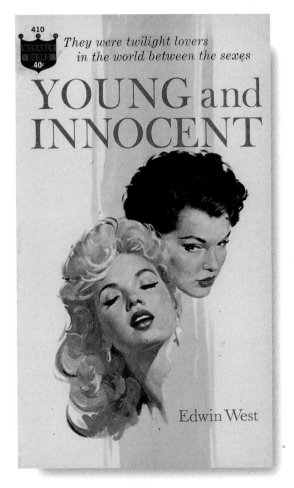

Midwood, 1964. Another spectacular cover by Robert Maguire, with the same models as on *Perfume and Pain*.

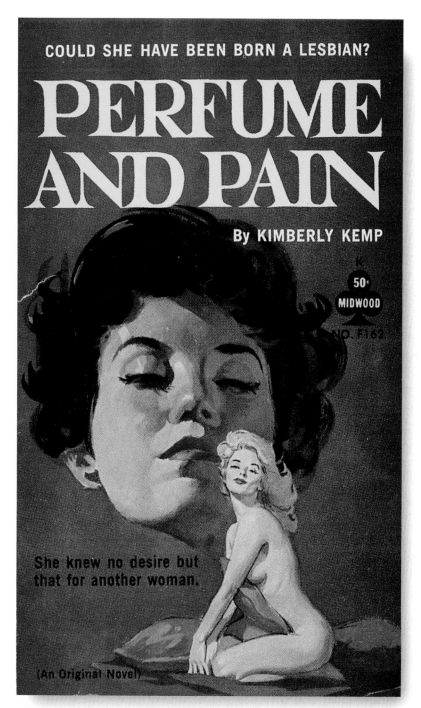

COULD SHE HAVE BEEN BORN A LESBIAN?

PERFUME AND PAIN

By KIMBERLY KEMP

K
50¢
MIDWOOD
NO. F162

She knew no desire but
that for another woman.

(An Original Novel)

Midwood, 1962. Cover painting by Robert Maguire. One of my favorites!

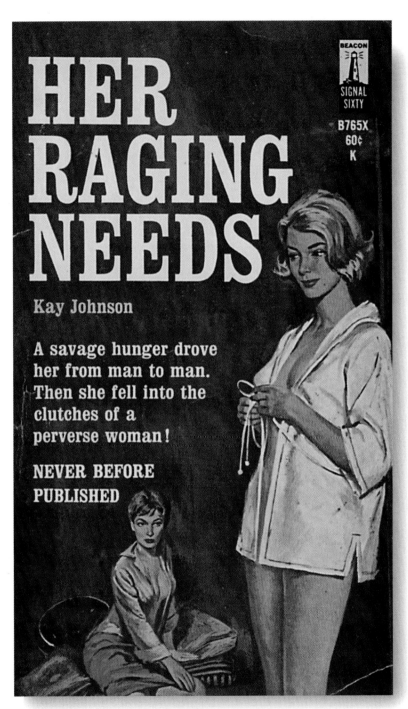

HER RAGING NEEDS

Kay Johnson

A savage hunger drove her from man to man. Then she fell into the clutches of a perverse woman!

NEVER BEFORE PUBLISHED

BEACON
SIGNAL SIXTY

B765X
60¢
K

Beacon, 1964.

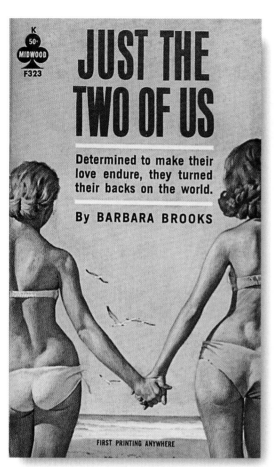

JUST THE TWO OF US

Determined to make their love endure, they turned their backs on the world.

By BARBARA BROOKS

FIRST PRINTING ANYWHERE

Midwood, 1963. Cover painting by Paul Rader.

"Liz had been cheating on her. Liz was becoming a tramp. A little chippy. A puta."

THE THIRD WAY

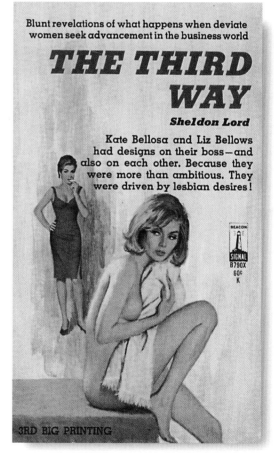

Blunt revelations of what happens when deviate women seek advancement in the business world

THE THIRD WAY

Sheldon Lord

Kate Bellosa and Liz Bellows had designs on their boss—and also on each other. Because they were more than ambitious. They were driven by lesbian desires!

3RD BIG PRINTING

Beacon Signal, 1964. Cover painting by Tom Miller.

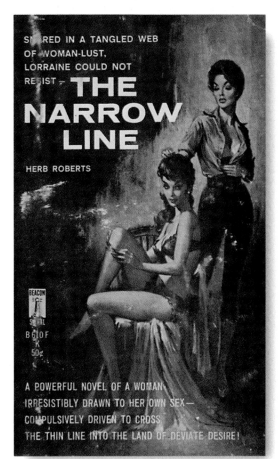

SNARED IN A TANGLED WEB OF WOMAN-LUST, LORRAINE COULD NOT RESIST—

THE NARROW LINE

HERB ROBERTS

BEACON SIGNAL
B610F
K
50¢

A POWERFUL NOVEL OF A WOMAN IRRESISTIBLY DRAWN TO HER OWN SEX—COMPULSIVELY DRIVEN TO CROSS THE THIN LINE INTO THE LAND OF DEVIATE DESIRE!

Beacon, 1963.

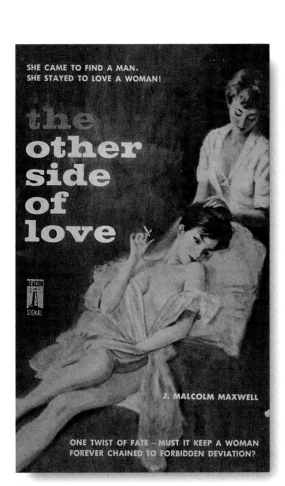

SHE CAME TO FIND A MAN.
SHE STAYED TO LOVE A WOMAN!

the other side of love

BEACON SIGNAL

J. MALCOLM MAXWELL

ONE TWIST OF FATE—MUST IT KEEP A WOMAN FOREVER CHAINED TO FORBIDDEN DEVIATION?

Beacon Signal, 1963.

"The place might be a Lesbian hangout, but I felt at home in it."

THE NARROW LINE

Bi, Bi, Love

Love triangles were a popular theme, especially for the sleaze publishers. Lesbianism seems even more exciting when it's a straying wife just out looking for a thrill. This bought into the notion that all any lesbian needed was the right man. All the better for the male reader to project himself into the fray!

the 3rd theme

50¢

by

MARCH HASTINGS

sleep meant dreams
of wild passion
beyond her control

Adult Reading

Newsstand Library, 1961. Cover painting by Robert Bonfils. Which one will she choose?

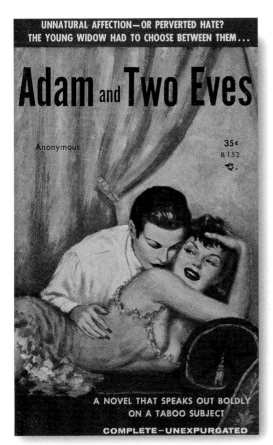

UNNATURAL AFFECTION—OR PERVERTED HATE?
THE YOUNG WIDOW HAD TO CHOOSE BETWEEN THEM...

Adam and Two Eves

Anonymous

35¢
B 152

A NOVEL THAT SPEAKS OUT BOLDLY
ON A TABOO SUBJECT

COMPLETE—UNEXPURGATED

Beacon, 1956. A butch with claws—Jungle Red!

"Suddenly I felt that I was in love with her—with him—with the two of them."
ADAM AND TWO EVES

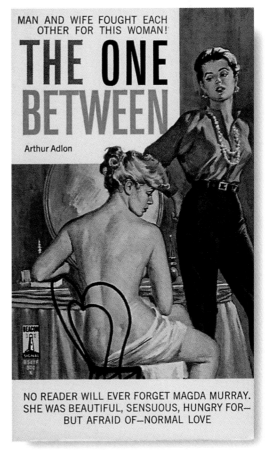

MAN AND WIFE FOUGHT EACH
OTHER FOR THIS WOMAN!

THE ONE
BETWEEN

Arthur Adlon

NO READER WILL EVER FORGET MAGDA MURRAY.
SHE WAS BEAUTIFUL, SENSUOUS, HUNGRY FOR—
BUT AFRAID OF—NORMAL LOVE

Beacon Signal, 1962. "Man and wife fought each other for this woman."

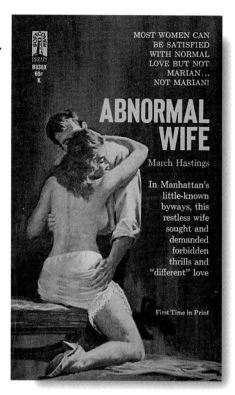

MOST WOMEN CAN
BE SATISFIED
WITH NORMAL
LOVE BUT NOT
MARIAN...
NOT MARIAN!

ABNORMAL WIFE

March Hastings

In Manhattan's
little-known
byways, this
restless wife
sought and
demanded
forbidden
thrills and
"different" love

First Time in Print

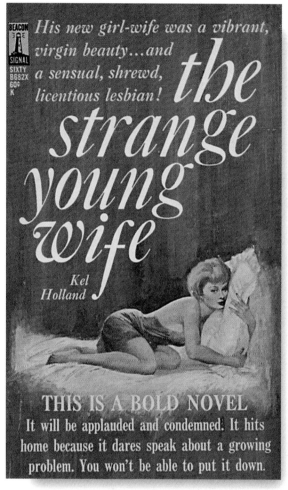

His new girl-wife was a vibrant, virgin beauty...and a sensual, shrewd, licentious lesbian!

the strange young wife

Kel Holland

THIS IS A BOLD NOVEL
It will be applauded and condemned. It hits home because it dares speak about a growing problem. You won't be able to put it down.

"To think that his own wife could find her pleasure that way, in the arms of another woman"

DEVIATE WIFE

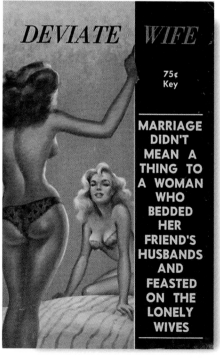

DEVIATE WIFE

75¢
Key

MARRIAGE
DIDN'T
MEAN A
THING TO
A WOMAN
WHO
BEDDED
HER
FRIEND'S
HUSBANDS
AND
FEASTED
ON THE
LONELY
WIVES

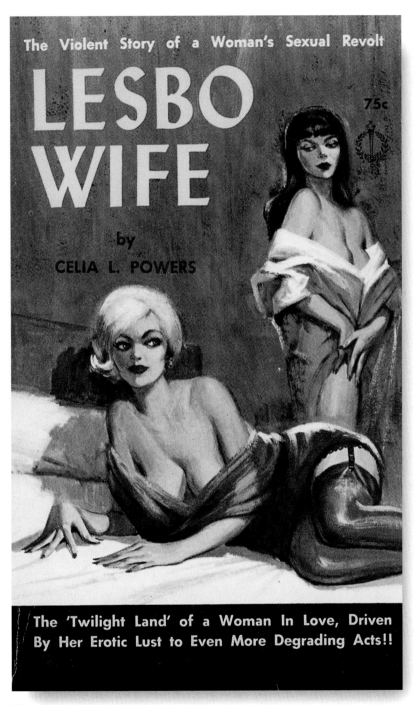

The Violent Story of a Woman's Sexual Revolt

LESBO WIFE

75c

by

CELIA L. POWERS

The 'Twilight Land' of a Woman In Love, Driven By Her Erotic Lust to Even More Degrading Acts!!

New Chariot, 1963.

KIMBERLY KEMP

COMING OUT PARTY

It was going to be a private affair — just the hostess, her husband, and their young houseguest.

50¢
MIDWOOD
32-448

FIRST PRINTING ANYWHERE

Midwood, 1965.

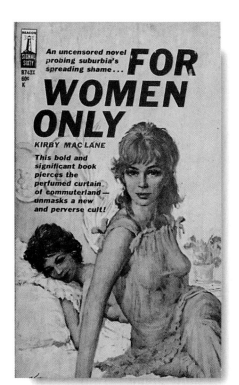

An uncensored novel probing suburbia's spreading shame...

FOR WOMEN ONLY

KIRBY MAC LANE

This bold and significant book pierces the perfumed curtain of commuterland — unmasks a new and perverse cult!

Beacon, 1964. Cover painting by Victor Olsen.

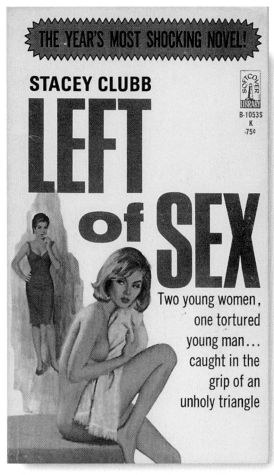

THE YEAR'S MOST SHOCKING NOVEL!

STACEY CLUBB

LEFT of SEX

Two young women, one tortured young man... caught in the grip of an unholy triangle

Softcover, 1967. Cover painting by Tom Miller. Reuse of art for *The Third Way*, p.115.

a novel of love's misfits...

this too is love

TOM VAIL

For many unhappy young wives like Janet, a woman like Rhonda is waiting — to teach a new kind of love!

Beacon, 1964. Cover painting by Ray App. Unhappy young wives.

Cleavage

Breasts are the first connection to our first relationship—our mothers—and some men can never forget that. Breasts have been so sexualized that their exposure is taboo. Even a small peek at their milky-white mounds is more erotically charged than full frontal nudity. These covers are some of the sexiest, and with good reason. The women represented here are presenting their breasts to the viewer as a blatant sexual invitation, a display of their wares. These women want sex, and are not afraid to ask for it!

A BOLD NEW NOVEL OF PERVERSITY

QUEER PATTERNS

Kay Addams

Beacon, 1959.

THEIRS WAS A PASSION
NO MAN COULD SHARE!

QUEER AFFAIR

by Carol Emery

THE NOVEL THAT DARES
TO TELL THE TRUTH ABOUT
A PERVERSE LOVE

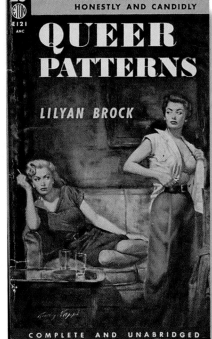

A DELICATE THEME, TREATED
HONESTLY AND CANDIDLY

QUEER PATTERNS

LILYAN BROCK

COMPLETE AND UNABRIDGED

Eton, 1952. Cover painting by Rudolph Nappi.

" . . . she recognized her danger.
She was on the brink of
total perversion."
QUEER AFFAIR

TWO WOMEN SHARING A LOVE THAT WAS

UNNATURAL

By SLOAN BRITTON

(an original novel)

A VIVID AND SEARCHING NOVEL OF FORBIDDEN
LOVE IN THE TWILIGHT WORLD OF THE THIRD SEX

Midwood, 1960. Cover painting by Paul Rader.

Meet The Most Gorgeous,
The Most Immoral, The Most
Depraved Woman Of Them All...

MEET MARILYN

By SLOANE BRITAIN

(an original novel)

NO. 52

Midwood, 1960. Cover painting by Al
Wagner.

GAY GIRL

Eve was so beautiful and open to love—but she
chose to seek satisfaction inside her own sex.

By JOAN ELLIS
author of "GAY SCENE"
and "IN THE SHADOWS"

FIRST PRINTING ANYWHERE

Midwood, 1962. Cover painting by Jerome Podwil.

The DOCTOR & the DIKE

K 40¢ MIDWOOD Y176

The Doctor knew all about women and he solved their sex problems in a most unique manner. His beautiful receptionist also had a problem — Lesbianism.

By JASON HYTES
Author of: "Rita" and "Pound of Flesh"

Midwood, 1962. Suicide in the end.

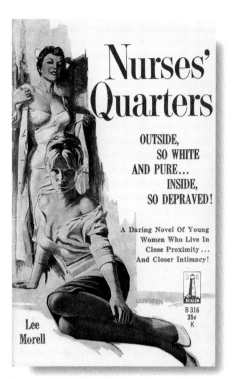

Nurses' Quarters

OUTSIDE, SO WHITE AND PURE... INSIDE, SO DEPRAVED!

A Daring Novel Of Young Women Who Live In Close Proximity... And Closer Intimacy!

BEACON
B 316
35¢
K

Lee Morell

Beacon, 1960.

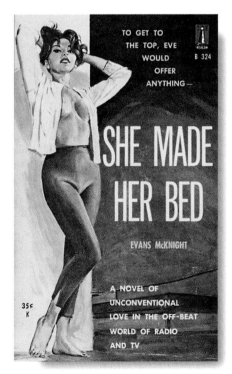

TO GET TO THE TOP, EVE WOULD OFFER ANYTHING —

BEACON
B 324

SHE MADE HER BED

EVANS McKNIGHT

A NOVEL OF UNCONVENTIONAL LOVE IN THE OFF-BEAT WORLD OF RADIO AND TV

35¢ K

Beacon,1960.

THE UNLOVED

A LUSH, SENSUOUS GIRL, SHE RAN IN SEARCH OF LOVE... AND FOUND THE SHOCKING TRUTH OF HER OWN ABNORMAL DESIRES

50¢ MIDWOOD NO. F110

by Peggy Swenson
Author of "THE BLONDE"

Midwood, 1961. Cover painting by Paul Rader. Written by Edward Geis.

A STORY THAT EXPOSES BROADWAY AS THE GAY WAY

LADDER OF FLESH

Broadway offered her a star studded ladder to climb to the top, but when she put her foot on the first rung she found herself climbing down a ladder of flesh into a cesspool of Lesbian depravity.

By SLOANE BRITAIN

K
50¢
MIDWOOD
F177

FIRST PRINTING ANYWHERE

Midwood, 1962. Cover painting by Victor Olsen.

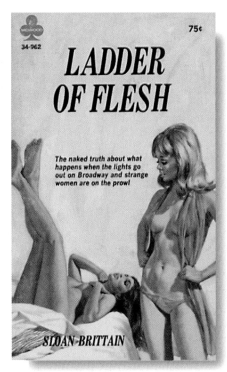

MIDWOOD
34-962

75¢

LADDER OF FLESH

The naked truth about what happens when the lights go out on Broadway and strange women are on the prowl!

SLOAN-BRITTAIN

Midwood, 1968.

MIDWOOD
32-484

Sloan Britain

FINDERS KEEPERS

She was a play-toy for a strange breed of older, wealthy women...women who knew her weakness and how to exploit it.

A MIDWOOD BOOK

(Originally entitled: LADDER OF FLESH)

Midwood, 1965. Cover painting by Paul Rader. Reprint of the 1962 book *Ladder of Flesh*.

"They fell upon each other with all the lust that was in them."

FINDERS KEEPERS

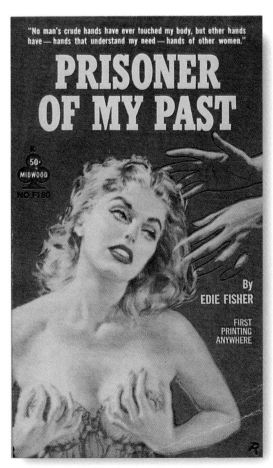

"No man's crude hands have ever touched my body, but other hands have — hands that understand my need — hands of other women."

PRISONER OF MY PAST

K 50¢
MIDWOOD
NO. F180

By
EDIE FISHER

FIRST
PRINTING
ANYWHERE

Midwood, 1962. Cover painting by Paul Rader.

"Marian Manchester, overt lesbian and insidious temptress"

MASK OF LESBOS

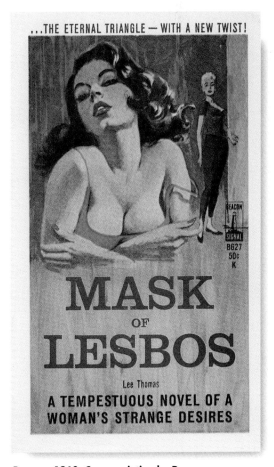

...THE ETERNAL TRIANGLE — WITH A NEW TWIST!

BEACON
SIGNAL
B627
50¢
K

MASK
OF
LESBOS

Lee Thomas

A TEMPESTUOUS NOVEL OF A
WOMAN'S STRANGE DESIRES

Beacon, 1963. Cover painting by Darcy.

Can a handsome, virile man come between two women who love each other passionately?

THE OTHER KIND

RICHARD VILLANOVA

THE FRANKLY TOLD STORY
OF A BEAUTIFUL YOUNG WOMAN
WHO HAD TO MAKE A CHOICE
BETWEEN CONVENTIONAL LOVE AND
THE DEVIATE KIND!

NEVER BEFORE PUBLISHED

Beacon Signal, 1963.

ARTHUR ADLON

The ODD Kind

THE REMARKABLE NOVEL THAT UN-
VEILS THE SLEEK AND EXPENSIVE
WORLD OF THE LESBIANS WHO MODEL
THE NEWEST FASHIONS IN PUBLIC
— AND PERFORM ANCIENT RITUALS IN
PRIVATE!

NEVER
BEFORE
PUBLISHED!

B492F
50¢ K

Beacon, 1962. Cover painting by Milo.

EVERY TIME A MAN HAD HER IT WAS RAPE,
BUT WITH OTHER WOMEN IT WAS LOVE.

Gay Scene

BY JOAN ELLIS
Author of: "In the Shadows"
and "Mulatto"

FIRST PRINTING ANYWHERE

K
50¢
MIDWOOD

NO. F169

Midwood, 1962.

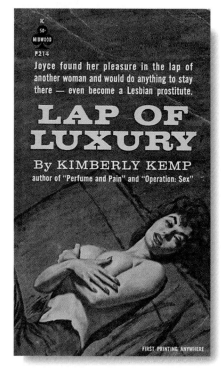

K
50¢
MIDWOOD

F214

Joyce found her pleasure in the lap of
another woman and would do anything to stay
there — even become a Lesbian prostitute.

LAP OF LUXURY

By KIMBERLY KEMP
author of "Perfume and Pain" and "Operation: Sex"

FIRST PRINTING ANYWHERE

Midwood, 1962. Cover painting by Paul Rader.

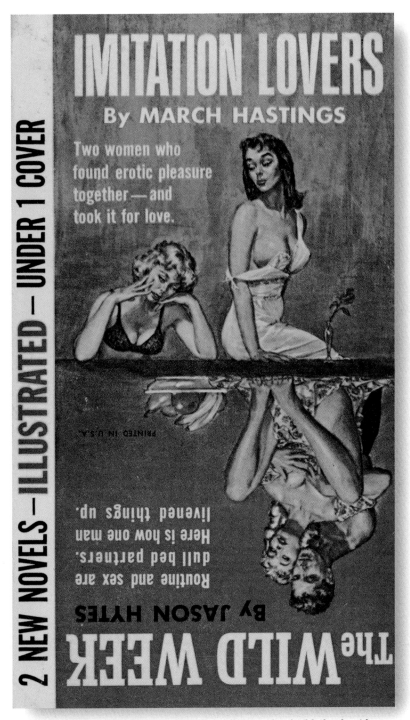

Midwood, 1963. A wonderful find for any collector—the double book with two pieces of cover art by Paul Rader and 8 black-and-white plates inside by Frank Frazetta.

Midwood, 1964. Cover painting by Paul Rader.

"... when can you admit to yourself you're a woman in love with another woman?"

THE GAY PARTNERS

Brandon House, 1964. Written by Edward Geis. Note the groovy Bertoia diamond chair.

Brandon House, 1965. Another Ed Geis book.

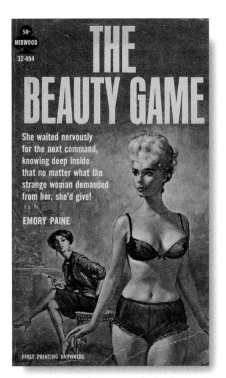

THE BEAUTY GAME

She waited nervously for the next command, knowing deep inside that no matter what the strange woman demanded from her, she'd give!

EMORY PAINE

FIRST PRINTING ANYWHERE

Midwood, 1965. Cover painting by Paul Rader.

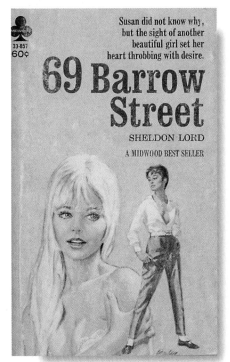

Susan did not know why, but the sight of another beautiful girl set her heart throbbing with desire.

69 Barrow Street

SHELDON LORD

A MIDWOOD BEST SELLER

Midwood, 1967. Cover painting by Paul Rader. Greenwich Village setting.

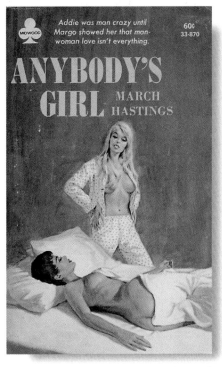

Addie was man crazy until Margo showed her that man-woman love isn't everything.

ANYBODY'S GIRL MARCH HASTINGS

Midwood, 1967. Cover painting by Paul Rader.

This is either the good stuff or the bad stuff, depending on how you look at it. Often poorly written in the most sensationalistic and exploitive prose, these books had no pretense of any literary merit. But their over-the-top covers and outrageous plot lines make these books a lot of fun!

Twisted Love and
Hateful Passion in
a Suspenseful Setting!

35¢

The
Queer Sisters

ANOTHER MASTERPIECE OF LUSTY ACTION
BY
STEVE HARRAGAN!

UNI
BOOK
43

B. Safran

Uni-Book, ND. Digest size. Cover painting by Bernard Safran. Drag queens or lesbians?

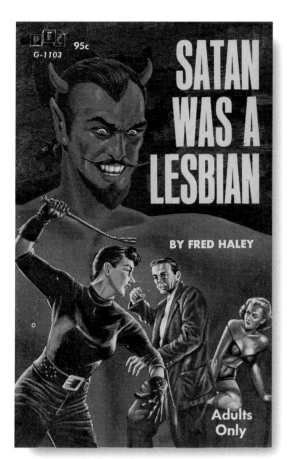

PEC, 1966. Cover painting by Doug Weaver, with obvious revisions of the painting used on *Satan's Daughter*. I don't quite see the point of the higher neckline or the gloves.

"'Love! You idiot! What's love got to do with this?'"

SATAN WAS
A LESBIAN

"... the world must someday recognize that Woman is the Superior Being!"

SATAN'S DAUGHTER

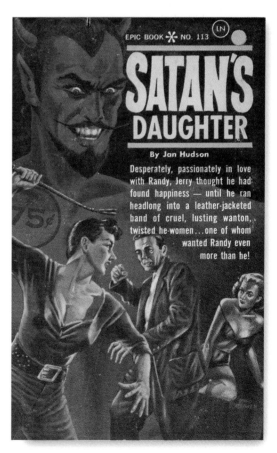

Epic Book, 1961. Cover painting by Doug Weaver. Reprint from a 1941 hardcover. Amazon S&M cult.

All Star, 1962.

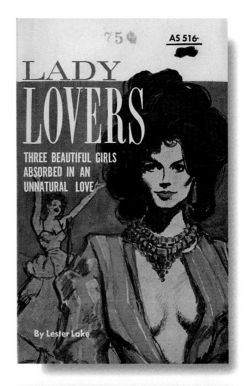

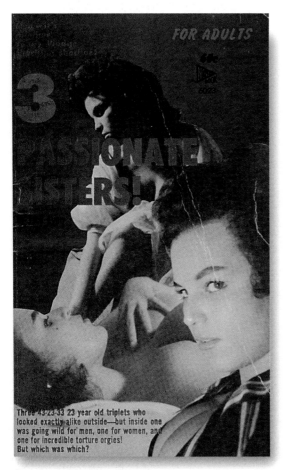

Novel, 1962. Very groovy photo cover.

"As you may know, Novel Books does not like lesbians—and thus does not like to publish books about them. We believe in a man as a hero....But once in a great while we make an exception."

MY LESBIAN LOVES

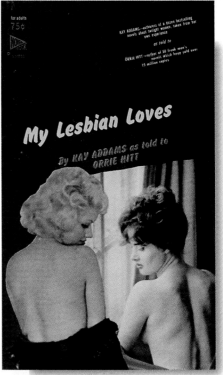

Novel, 1964.

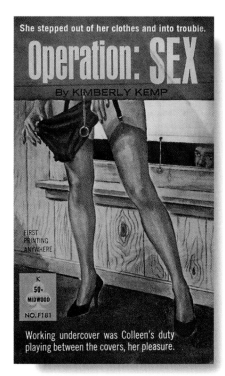

She stepped out of her clothes and into trouble.

Operation: SEX

By KIMBERLY KEMP

FIRST
PRINTING
ANYWHERE

K
50¢
MIDWOOD
NO. F181

Working undercover was Colleen's duty playing between the covers, her pleasure.

Midwood, 1962. Cover painting by Paul Rader.

THEY CALL ME

LEZ

60¢

"This Book Will Shock You!

It will force you into that strange, often perverted, half-world between the sexes. It will open your eyes to forbidden passions, and it *may* open your heart to a searing social problem."
Sheldon W. Fencer, M.D.

by JoAnn Radelli

Paradiso, 1963.

95¢

The
Third Sex Syndrome

by March Hastings

TWO complete full length novels

Her doctor had said: "there is in some women a latent force for sexual deviation, deep and controlled . . . yours has come to the surface."

Dollar Double, 1962. Cover painting by Robert Bonfils. Two books for a buck.

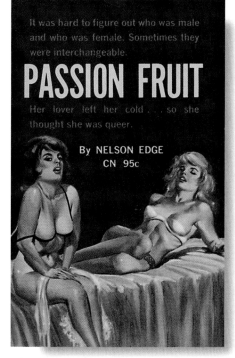

It was hard to figure out who was male and who was female. Sometimes they were interchangeable.

PASSION FRUIT

Her lover left her cold . . . so she thought she was queer.

By NELSON EDGE
CN 95c

All Star, ND. Cover painting by John Healy.

143

A GAY, GAY WORLD

The bizarre world of the outcast sex – women who seek forbidden pleasures with other women . . .

Key   75¢

Raven, 1963. Cover painting by John Healy.

75¢
ADULTS
ONLY

MAN HATER

She hated men and turned to a lesbian for comfort

FRANCE

FIRST
AMERICAN
PRINTING

France, 1963.

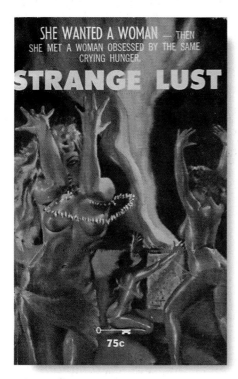

SHE WANTED A WOMAN — THEN
SHE MET A WOMAN OBSESSED BY THE SAME
CRYING HUNGER.

STRANGE LUST

75c

Private Editions, 1963.

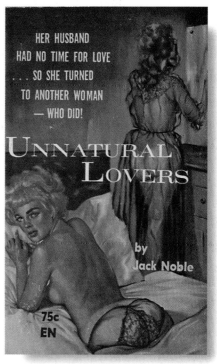

HER HUSBAND
HAD NO TIME FOR LOVE
. . . SO SHE TURNED
TO ANOTHER WOMAN
— WHO DID!

UNNATURAL LOVERS

by
Jack Noble

75c
EN

Private Editions, 1963. Cover painting by John Healy.

145

751-S

LESBIAN NURSE

75c

BENEATH HER CALM
EFFICIENCY RAGED
FIRES OF PERVERTED
LUST

...ANK SHIELD

Playtime, 1965.

"Willie fell easy prey to the
unique caresses of lesbian
love. She was a more than
willing convert."

LESBIAN NURSE

French Line 7

95c

By Appointment Only:
SEX SALON

BY JULIE ROWE

THE FINEST IN
ADULT READING

PEC, French Line, 1966.

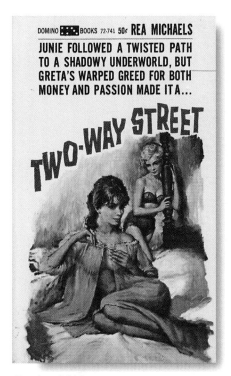

DOMINO BOOKS 72-741 50¢ **REA MICHAELS**

JUNIE FOLLOWED A TWISTED PATH TO A SHADOWY UNDERWORLD, BUT GRETA'S WARPED GREED FOR BOTH MONEY AND PASSION MADE IT A...

TWO-WAY STREET

Domino, 1964.

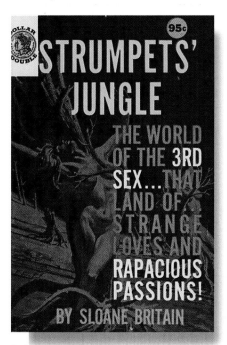

95¢

STRUMPETS' JUNGLE

THE WORLD OF THE 3RD SEX... THAT LAND OF STRANGE LOVES AND RAPACIOUS PASSIONS!

BY SLOANE BRITAIN

Dollar Double, 1966. Cover painting by Robert Bonfils.

"Why don't you learn from me— learn what it's like to have a woman make love to you?"

LESBIAN ORGIES

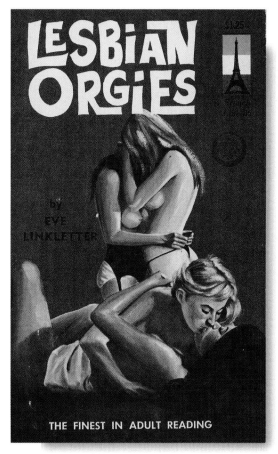

$1.25

LESBIAN ORGIES

BY EVE LINKLETTER

THE FINEST IN ADULT READING

PEC, French Line, 1968.

moment
of
desire

60¢

It was a wild, orgiastic party—the kind where anything goes and your big competition is straight from Les land.

BY FLETCHER BENNETT

Playtime, ND. Cover painting by Bonfils

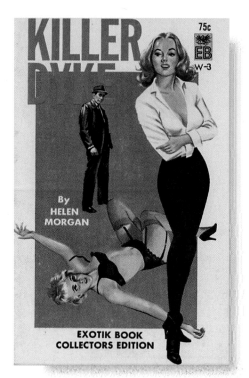

KILLER
DYKE

75c

EB
W-3

By
HELEN
MORGAN

EXOTIK BOOK
COLLECTORS EDITION

Exotik Book, 1964.

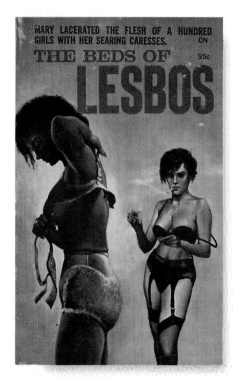

MARY LACERATED THE FLESH OF A HUNDRED GIRLS WITH HER SEARING CARESSES.
CN

THE BEDS OF
LESBOS

95c

All Star, 1964. Ugh!

BRANDON 75c

QUEER
BEACH

BY PEGGY SWENSON

It is like a beautiful spider's web: waiting to lure innocent strangers into the perverted world from which there is no possible escape!

Brandon House, 1964. Written by Edward Geis, this time as Peggy Swenson.

148

LESBIAN LURE

by Peggy Swanson

From a nightmare of brutal lust to a wildly exciting mating, a strange, forbidden love. "Outcast!" they screamed. "Abnormal!" but desire closed her ears.

Playtime, 1964. Written by Edward Geis, as Peggy Swanson. Geis used both Swanson and Swenson as pseudonyms, probably due to a typo on one of his covers.

Bibliography

Books

Bonn, Thomas L. *Under Cover.* New York: Penguin, 1982. (o/p)

> Excellent overview of the paperback in America, with tips on collecting and color inserts of covers.

Collectable Vintage Paperbacks at Auction. Compiled by Gorgon Books. Holbrook, NY: Gorgon Books, 1995.

> Comparative prices from various paperback auctions. Gives guidelines for prices, especially price differences between top and lesser conditions.

Damon, Gene, Jan Watson and Robin Jordan. *The Lesbian in Literature,* 2nd ed. Reno: The Ladder, 1975.

> (o/p) An earlier edition of Grier.

Faderman, Lillian. *Odd Girls and Twilight Lovers.* New York: Columbia University Press, 1991.

> The essential history of lesbians in America, from romantic friendships to the nineties.

Foster, Jeannette H. *Sex Variant Women in Literature.* Tallahassee: Naiad, 1985.

> Scholarly bibliography commenting on lesbian aspects in literature from Sappho to the fifties.

Grier, Barbara. *The Lesbian in Literature,* 3rd ed. Tallahassee: Naiad, 1981.

> Lesbian bibliography with rating system for lesbian content and quality. Useful but incomplete.

Hancer, Kevin. *The Paperback Price Guide.* Edina, MN: Overstreet, 1980. (o/p)

> Handy illustrated guide.

Huxford, Bob, and Sharon Huxford. *Huxford's Paperback Value Guide.* Paducah, KY: Collector Books, 1994.

> Compilation of prices from auctions and lists.

Kuda, Marie J. *Women Loving Women.* Chicago: Lavender Press, 1974.

> An early lesbian bibliography.

McGarry, Molly, and Fred Wasserman. *Becoming Visible.* New York: Penguin Studio, 1998.

> Based on an exhibit at The New York Public Library, a densely illustrated history of homosexuality in twentieth-century America.

Schreuders, Piet. *Paperbacks, U.S.A.* San Diego: Blue Dolphin, 1981. (o/p)

> An illustrated history with information on publishers and cover artists.

Server, Lee. *Over My Dead Body.* San Fransisco: Chronicle, 1994.

> Wonderful book about vintage paperbacks, with 100 covers illustrated.

Summers, Claude J., ed. *Gay and Lesbian Literary Heritage.* New York: Holt, 1997.

> Comprehensive overview of gay/lesbian literature.

Warren, Jon. *The Official Price Guide: Paperbacks.* New York: House of Collectables, 1991.

> Prices out of date, but is a good reference for cover attributions.

Articles

Hunsanger, Kevin. "Under Wraps: Collecting Vintage Paperbacks." *Biblio,* Vol. 2, No. 5 (May 1997): 26-31.

Pressman, Jeffrey Lee. "Lesbiana: A Checklist of Significant Post-War Lesbian Literature in the Mass-Market Paperback." *Books Are Everything,* Vol. 4, No. 4 (Dec. 1991): 32-47.

Lovisi, Gary. "An Interview with Marijane Meaker: The Woman Behind Vin Packer and Ann Aldrich." *Paperback Parade,* 47 (Feb. 1997): 16-22.

———. "The Paperbacks of Vin Packer and Ann Aldrich." Ibid., 16-22.

Miller, Laurence. "A 'Golden Age' of Gay and Lesbian Literature in Mainstream Mass-Market Paperbacks." *Paperback Parade,* 47 (Feb. 1997): 37-66.

———. "Adult-Oriented Gay and Lesbian Paperbacks During the Golden Age." *Paperback Parade,* 49 (Dec. 1997): 26-41.

———. "A Selected List of Adult-Oriented Titles." Ibid.

Film

Forbidden Love: The Unashamed Stories of Lesbian Lives, 1992, 85 min. Aerlyn Weissman and Lynne Ferme, directors; produced by the National Film Board of Canada.
    Excellent documentary with interviews of women spliced with tableaux from vintage novels.

Resources

Book Dealers Specializing in Vintage Paperbacks and Pulps

Books Are Everything, R. C. and Elwanda Holland—606-624-9176, 302 Martin Drive, Richmond, KY 40475-3505

Chris Eckhoff—98 Pierrepont St., Brooklyn, NY 11201
Issues lists and specializes in sleaze.

Kayo Books—415-749-0554, 814 Post St., San Francisco, CA 94109

Thomas M. Lesser, Bookseller—818-249-3844

Mark's Vintage Paperbacks—812-476-1967, 2900 Bergdolt Rd., Evansville, IN 47711

Modern Age Books, Jeff Canja—517-487-9313, P.O. Box 325, East Lansing, MI 48826
Issues lists and telephone auctions.

Olde Current Books, Daniel P. Shay—904-672-8998, 356 Putnam Ave., Ormond Beach, FL 32174

Pandora's Books—204-324-8548, Box 54, Neche, ND 58265

Jeffrey Lee Pressman—412-441-3942, 837 N. St. Clair St., #2, Pittsburgh, PA 15206

River Oaks Books, Nick and Barbara Bogdon—207-897-3734, R.R. 2, Box 5505, Jay, ME 04239

On-Line Stores Specializing in Vintage Paperbacks

Books Are Everything—http://www.booksareeverything.com/index.html
R. C. and Elwanda Holland's site. Lists books by publisher.

Cover Art Vintage Paperback and Rare Books—http://members.tripod.com/~ggabooks/
Store with scans of covers of books for sale. Long download time.

Cybertiques—http://www.nemaine.com:80/cybertiques/index.html

Dime Box Books—http://www.dimeboxbooks.com

Everglades—http://www.evergladesbookcompany.com

Kayo Books—http://www.sfo.com/~kayo/index.html

Mark's Vintage Paperbacks—http://hometown.aol.com/markB45375/Mark.htm

The Men's Room—http://www.arrowweb.net/frame/mensroom.htm
Store with cover art and an article entitled "The Lure of the Paperback Lesbian."

Olde Current Books, Daniel P. Shay—http://members.aol.com/peakmyster/aolwp.htm

Pandora's Books—http://www.mbnet.mb.ca/pandora/
Category lists with links to others.

Powell's Books—http://www.powells.com
Huge Seattle-based used and rare book store. As well as searches, you can browse by category, and it has a large gay/lesbian studies section.

On-Line Auction Services

E-bay—http://www.ebay.com
Collectors' nirvana! Prices tend to run high if there's competition. A hotly contested auction I was involved in for the book Satan Was a Lesbian went for over $100! (I paid $15 at a book show soon after.) Easiest way to find vintage paperbacks is to search under title for "vintage, paperback." Add "lesbian" as a modifier if you want to get specific.

On-Line Vintage Paperback Cover Art Galleries

Cybertiques Gallery of Covers—http://www.nemaine.com:80/cybertiques/gallery.html

Gallery of Cover Art—http://sfo.com/~kayo/covers.html

Kate's Library—http://www.dnai.com/~lakate/

Amazing gallery of cover art, mostly gang and torture art.

Lurid Paperback of the Week—http://www.nwrain.com/~monlux/LuridPaperbackofWeek.html

Updated weekly, with covers and commentary and links to other sites.

Naughty Novels—http://www.grrl.com/sleaze.html

Excellent site! Tons of covers, including Good Girl Art and Bad Girl Art, with some lesbiana thrown in.

Paperback and Pulp Waystation—http://www.geocities.com/Area51/cavern/5792

Links to everything, and gallery.

Paperback Cover Art Display—http://ils.unc.edu/rarebooks/illustrators.html

Cover art and information on seven illustrators. Sponsored by the University of North Carolina.

Pulp Fiction Paperback Covers—http://www.joebates.com/nostalgia/pulp1.htm

E-zines

Grrl—http://grrl.com/main.html

Pulp and Paperback Waystation—http://www.geocities.com/Area51/cavern/5792

Unbelievable site with articles and links to everything!

Tawdry Town—http://www.users.interport.net/~xcentrik

Site with cover art, articles and links.

Multidealer On-Line Book Searches

Advanced Book Exchange—http://www.abe.com

Bibliocity—http://www.bibliocity.com

International book dealers.

BiblioFind—http://www.bibliofind.com

Hosts 3000 worldwide dealers!

Interloc—http://www.interloc.com/

MX Bookfinder—http://www.mxbf.com/

Searches some other search sites on this list in one go!

Publications

Paperback Parade, edited by Gary Lovisi—Gryphon Publications, P.O. Box 209, Brooklyn, NY 11228

$8 per issue, or $35 for 5-issue subscription.

Index

*Denotes cover artist

Abby, Alain, 108
Abnormal Wife, March Hastings, 122
Adam and Two Eves, Anon., 121
Addams, Kay, 95, 128, 142
Adlon, Arthur, 64, 97, 111, 121, 134
Aldrich, Ann *(Marijane Meaker)*, 50, 51
Amanda, Paula Christian, 59
American Sexual Behavior, Ernst and Roth, 84
Anybody's Girl, March Hastings, 137
*App, Ray, 125
Avallone, Mike, 31

Bannon, Ann, 47, 54, 55
Beauchamp, Loren *(Robert Silverberg)*, 68
Beauty Game, The, Emory Paine, 137
Beds of Lesbos, The, 148
Beebo Brinker, Ann Bannon, 55
Bennet, Fletcher, 148
Bitter Love, Don King, 94
Bligh, Norman, 106
Block, Lawence, *as Andrew Shaw*, 34
*Bonfils, Robert, 120, 143, 147, 148
Born Innocent, Creighton Brown Burnham, 32
Bradley, Marion Zimmer, *as Miriam Gardner*, 58, 67
Britain, Sloane, 88, 105, 129, 132, 147
Britton, Sloan, 129
Brock, Lilyan, 128
Brooks, Barbara, 115
*Brooks, Walter, 84
Burnham, Creighton Brown, 32
Burns, Vincent E., 32, 33
By Love Depraved, Arthur Adlon, 97

Carol in a Thousand Cities, Ann Aldrich, ed., 51
Cassill, R.V., 37
Christian, Paula, 53, 59

City of Women, Nancy Morgan, 36, 37
Clubb, Stacey, 125
Coming Out Party, Kimberly Kemp, 124
Cooper, Pauline, 43
Craig, D.W., 136
Craigin, Elisabeth, 76

Damned One, The, Guy des Cars, 80, 81
Dangerous Games, The, Tereska Torres, 48
*Darcy, 35, 97, 106, 111, 133
Dean, Ralph, 105
Degraded Women, James Harvey, 31
des Cars, Guy, 80, 81
*Desoto, Rafael M., 58
Deviate Wife, 122
Diana, Diana Fredericks, 81
Doctor & the Dike, The, Jason Hytes, 131
Doctor of Lesbos, Anthony Gordon, 88
Dormitory Women, R.V. Cassill, 37
Dumont, Jessie, 112

Edge of Twilight, Paula Christian, 53
Edge, Nelson, 143
Edmunds, Ronnie, 145
Either Is Love, Elisabeth Craigin, 76
Ellis, Joan *(F. C. Kneller)*, 129, 134
Emery, Carol, 128
Ernst, Morris, and David Roth, 84
Evil Friendship, The, Vin Packer, 59

Faderman, Jr., Edwin, *as Edwina Mark*, 81
Female Convict, Vincent E. Burns, 32, 33
Finders Keepers, Sloan Britain, 132
First Person 3rd Sex, Sloan Britain, 105
Fisher, Edie, 133
Flora, Fletcher, 62
Foran, Tom, 100
Forbidden, J. C. Priest, 94
For Women Only, Kirby Mac Lane, 125
Fredericks, Diana, 81

Gardner, Miriam (Marion Zimmer Bradley), 58, 67
Gay, Gay World, A, Ronnie Edmunds, 145
Gay Girl, Joan Ellis. 129
Gay Partners, The, Peggy Swenson, 136
Gay Scene, Joan Ellis, 134
Geis, Edward,
    as Peggy Swanson, 40, 149
    as Peggy Swenson, 38, 131, 136, 137, 148
Gerould, Christopher, 84
Girls' Dormitory, Orrie Hitt, 38
Girls in 3-B, The, Valerie Taylor, 56
Gold, R.C., 145
Gordon, Anthony, 88
Gregory, Paul, 98

Haley, Fred, 141
Hall, Radclyffe, 79
Harragan, Steve, 140
Harris, Sara, 37
Harvey, James, 31
Hastings, March, 43, 53, 59, 120, 122, 135, 137, 143
*Healy, John, 143, 145
Heat of the Day, The, March Hastings, 43
Henry, Joan, 30
Her Raging Needs, Kay Johnson, 114
Her Woman, Richard Villanova, 108
Highsmith, Patricia, as Claire Morgan, 75
Hitt, Orrie, 38, 104
Holk, Agnete, 64
Holland, Kel, 122
Holliday, Don, 43
House of Fury, Felice Swados, 29
Hudson, Jan, 141
*Hulings, Clark, 37
Hytes, Jason, 131

I Am a Woman, Ann Bannon, 54
Imitation Lovers, March Hastings, 135
Intimate, Martha Marsden, 107
Into the Fire, Paul V. Russo, 41
I Prefer Girls, Jessie Dumont, 112

Johnson, Kay, 114
Journey to a Woman, Ann Bannon, 54

Just the Two of Us, Barbara Brooks, 115

Kemp, Kimberly, 43, 113, 124, 134, 143
Killer Dyke, Helen Morgan, 148
King, Don, 94
Kneller, F.C., as Joan Ellis, 129, 134
Krich, A.M., 84

Ladder of Flesh, Sloan Britain, 132
Lady Lovers, Lester Lake, 142
Lake, Lester, 142
Lap of Luxury, Kimberly Kemp, 134
Lee, Marjorie, 73
Left of Sex, Stacey Clubb, 125
Lesbian Lure, Peggy Swanson, 149
Lesbian Nurse, Frank Shield, 146
Lesbian Orgies, Eve Linkletter, 147
Lesbian in Our Society, The, W. D. Sprague, 86
Lesbo Wife, Celia Powers, 123
*Lesser, Ronnie, 64
Libido Beach, Alain Abby, 108
Linkletter, Eve, 147
Lion House, The, Marjorie Lee, 73
Lord, Sheldon, 41, 97, 110, 115, 137

*McGinnis, Robert, 55, 73
McKnight, Evans, 131
Mac Lane, Kirby, 125
*Maguire, Robert, 29, 31, 32, 33, 62, 69, 89, 112, 113
Man Hater, R. C. Gold, 145
Marchal, Lucie, 73
Mark, Edwina (Edwin Faderman, Jr.), 81
Marr, Reed, 31
Marriage, The, Ann Bannon, 54
Marsden, Martha, 107
Marta, Sheldon Lord, 110
Martin, Kay, 106
Mask of Lesbos, Lee Thomas, 133
Maxwell, J. Malcolm, 117
Mayo, Dallas, 110
Meaker, Marijane,
    as Ann Aldrich, 50, 51
    as Vin Packer, 46, 47, 59
Meet Marilyn, Sloane Britain, 129

Mesh, The, Lucie Marchal, 73
*Micarelli, 38, 100
Michaels, Rea, 147
*Miller, Tom, 67, 76, 115, 125
*Milo, 134
Mimi, Orrie Hitt, 104
Moment of Desire, Fletcher Bennet, 148
Morell, Lee, 131
Morgan, Claire (Patricia Highsmith), 75
Morgan, Helen, 148
Morgan, Nancy, 36, 37
Morrison, Ray, 35
Mortimer, Lee, 84
My Lesbian Loves, Kay Addams, 142

*Nappi, Rudolph, 81, 128
Narrow Line, The, Herb Roberts, 117
Noble, Jack, 145
Norday, Michael, 69, 100, 101
Nurses' Quarters, Lee Morell, 131

Odd Girl Out, Ann Bannon, 47
Odd Kind, The, Arthur Adlon, 111, 134
Odd Ones, The, Edwina Mark, 81
Of Shame and Joy, Sheldon Lord, 97
Olive Branch, The, Pauline Cooper, 43
*Olsen, Victor, 64, 107, 125, 132
One Between, The, Arthur Adlon, 121
One Kind of Woman, Ralph Dean, 105
Only in Secret, D. W. Craig, 136
Operation: Sex, Kimberly Kemp, 143
Other Kind, The, Richard Villanova, 134
Other Side of Love, The, J. Malcolm Maxwell, 117

Packer, Vin (Marijane Meaker), 46, 47, 59
Paine, Emory, 137
Pajama Party, Peggy Swenson, 38
Pamela's Sweet Agony, Peggy Swenson, 137
Park, Jordan, 37
Passion Fruit, Nelson Edge, 143
Path Between, The, Jay Warren, 108
Perfume & Pain, Kimberly Kemp, 113
*Phillips, Barye, 28, 29, 31, 36, 37, 46, 47, 75, 108
*Podwil, Jerome, 129
Powers, Celia, 123

Preston, Lillian, 89
Price of Salt, The, Claire Morgan, 75
Price Was Perversity, The, Paul Gregory, 98
Priest, J.C., 38, 94
Prisoner of My Past, Edie Fisher, 133
Pritchard, Janet, 92, 93
Private Party, Kimberly Kemp, 43
Private School, J. C. Priest, 38

Queer Affair, Carol Emery, 128
Queer Beach, Peggy Swenson, 148
Queer Patterns, Kay Addams, 128
Queer Patterns, Lilyan Brock, 128
Queer Sisters, The, Steve Harragan, 140

Radcliff, Jo Ann, 143
*Rader, Paul, 38, 59, 68, 88, 97, 98, 108, 110, 115, 129, 131, 132, 133, 134, 135, 136, 137, 143
Reformatory Girls, Ray Morrison, 35
Reform School Girls, Andrew Shaw, 34
Robertiello, Richard, 85
Roberts, Herb, 117
Roberts, Monica, 100
Rollins, Rhonda, 69
*Rossi, Al, 99
Rowe, Julie, 146
Russo, Paul V., 41

*Safran, Bernard, 63, 140
Salem, Randy, 98, 99, 111
Satan's Daughter, Jan Hudson, 141
Satan Was a Lesbian, Fred Haley, 141
Scorpion, The, A. E. Weirauch, 72
Sex Between, The, Randy Salem, 111
Sex Habits of Single Women, Lillian Preston, 89
Sex Salon, Julie Rowe, 146
Sex in the Shadows, Randy Salem, 99
Sexual Practices of American Women, Christopher Gerould, 84
Shaw, Andrew (Lawrence Block), 34
She Made Her Bed, Evans McKnight, 131
Sherwood, Danni, 69
Shield, Frank, 146
Silverberg, Robert, as Loren Beauchamp, 68

Sinful Desires, Florence Stonebraker, 100
Sin School, Don Holliday, 43
Sisterhood, The, Sheldon Lord, 41
Sisters, The, Norman Bligh, 106
69 Barrow Street, Sheldon Lord, 137
Sorority House, Jordan Park, 37
So Strange a Love, Danni Sherwood, 69
Sprague, W.D., 86
Spring Fire, Vin Packer, 46, 47
*Stone, David, 76
Stonebraker, Florence, 63, 100
Strange Delights, Loren Beauchamp, 68
Strange Friends, Agnete Holk, 64
Strange Lust, 145
Strange Passions, Florence Stonebraker,
    63
Strange Path, The, Gale Wilhelm, 78
Stranger on Lesbos, Valerie Taylor, 57
Strange Seduction, Arthur Adlon, 64
Strange Sisters, Fletcher Flora, 62
Strange Sisters, Robert Turner, 65
Strange Thirsts, Michael Norday, 69
Strange Trio, The, Rhonda Rollins, 69
Strange Women, Miriam Gardner, 67
Strange Young Wife, Kel Holland, 122
Strumpets' Jungle, Sloane Britain, 147
Suzy and Vera, Peggy Swanson, 40
Swados, Felice, 29
Swanson, Peggy, 40, 149
Swenson, Peggy, 38, 131, 136, 137, 148

Taylor, Valerie, 48, 56, 57
Tender Torment, Randy Salem, 98
They Call Me Lez, Jo Ann Radcliff, 143
Thomas, Lee, 133
3 Passionate Sisters, 142
Three Women, March Hastings, 53
Third Sex Syndrome, March Hastings, 143
3rd Theme, The, March Hastings, 120
Third Way, The, Sheldon Lord, 115
This Too Is Love, Tom Vail, 125
Torres, Tereska, 28, 29, 48
Troubled Sex, The, Carlson Wade, 87
Turner, Robert, 65
21 Gay Street, Sheldon Lord, 110

Twilight Lovers, Miriam Gardner, 58
Twisted Ones, The, Tom Foran, 100
Two-Way Street, Rea Michaels, 147

Unashamed, The, March Hastings, 59
Unloved, The, Peggy Swenson, 131
Unnatural, Sloan Britton, 129
Unnatural Lovers, Jack Noble, 145

Vail, Tom, 125
Villanova, Richard, 108, 134
Voluptuous Voyage, Dallas Mayo, 110
Voyage from Lesbos, Richard Robertiello, 85

Wade, Carlson, 87
*Wagner, Al, 129
Warped, Michael Norday, 100, 101
Warped Desire, Kay Addams, 95
Warped Women, Janet Pritchard, 92, 93
Warren, Jay, 108
Wayward Ones, The, Sara Harris, 37
*Weaver, Doug, 141
Weirauch, A. E. (Anna Elisabet), 72
Well of Loneliness, The, Radclyffe Hall, 79
West, Edwin *(Donald E. Westlake),* 112
Westlake, Donald E., *as Edwin West,* 112
We Too Are Drifting, Gale Wilhelm, 76
We, Too, Must Love, Ann Aldrich, 51
We Walk Alone, Ann Aldrich, 50
Whispered Sex, The, Kay Martin, 106
Whisper Their Love, Valerie Taylor, 48
Wilhelm, Gale, 76, 78
Woman of Darkness, Monica Roberts, 100
Woman Doctor, Sloane Britain, 88
Women, A. M. Krich, ed., 84
Women Confidential, Lee Mortimer, 84
Women in Prison, Mike Avallone, 31
Women in Prison, Joan Henry, 30
Women in the Shadows, Ann Bannon, 54
Women's Barracks, Tereska Torres, 28, 29
Women Without Men, Reed Marr, 31

Young and Innocent, Edwin West, 112

*Ziel, George, 80, 81

ACKNOWLEDGMENTS

As an obsessive collector, I would like to thank my love, Stephanie Schwartz, for putting up with the many forays to antiquarian book fairs and paperback expos, as well as to antique shows of all shapes and sizes. And also for having a sense of humor about the seemingly endless e-bay purchases that appear on our doorstep.

At Viking, I would like to thank Christopher Sweet, Roni Axelrod and Tory Klose for their help in putting this book together. A special group hug to my harem, Alice, Betty, Francesca, Kathy, Lorrelle and Mia.

I am especially indebted to Ann Bannon, whose books have touched many people, and for her invaluable help and enthusiasm for my project. And also to Chris Eckhoff, without whose vast knowledge of lesbiana this book would not be complete; and to Gary Lovisi for all his help.